Musical Mysteries

by
Kathleen Fergusson

illustrated by
Gerald Melton

Cover by Gerald Melton
Copyright © Good Apple, Inc., 1985
ISBN No. 0-86653-282-X
Printing No. 987654

GOOD APPLE, INC.
BOX 299
CARTHAGE, IL 62321-0299

Dedicated to PAT
A librarian who knows how to encourage
and how to help and has never had a book
dedicated to her

and also to ESTELLE
whose musical knowledge and perceptive,
humorous criticism was so very valuable
all of the time

TABLE OF CONTENTS

And Now to Begin . . .

Suggestions and Directions

1. In solving the word searches, the words may go up, down, forward or backward, and in either direction on the diagonal. After all of the words have been found, some letters will remain unused; these will form the Mystery Word. In looking for these, start on the top line and look from left to right . . . like reading, progressing from line to line. The letters may sometimes be lines or spaces apart, but if you find one, then another and another, the Mystery Word will emerge.

   A successful method of using these word searches is letting two children work together (three at the most), one child seems to encourage the other. If a ''see through'' felt pen is used, the used letters may be clearly seen; unused letters and words that have been found stand out clearly. If music on the subject (or by the subject) of the word search has been studied, these compositions might be played while the children are working on the word search. It has been known to bring an appreciative ''play that again, please!''

2. The time frame was planned to bridge the known to the unknown. A well-known or famous event in the United States is tied to a happening in the life of the word search subject. This is an excellent time to discuss them both, tying together music and social studies. See the section ''Making the Subject Come Alive'' for activities to encourage the children to think deeper about the subject.

3. In the Number Word Games, the clues must be answered first and spelled correctly. Look back to the fact section for the answers and spellings. The letters of the answers are placed on the blank lines after the clues; under each blank line is a number. After the letter is placed on the blank line, find the same number throughout the story and write the same letter above it. Words will result as more clues are answered and the letters placed above the numbers . . . and the same letters are placed above the same number throughout the story. The completed story will yield further information about the subject of the word search.

4. The Cryptic Stories are alphabet substitution stories. One letter of the alphabet is substituted for another letter. Throughout the story the same letter will be substituted; it is a code that is a challenge to break. Each story will have a different letter substitution code. A letter by itself is usually an *I* or an *A.* Frequently appearing two-letter words might be *as, it, or* or *by.* Some often used three-letter words might be *and, the* or *are.* The clues given usually give a good start. The Challenger Cryptic Stories are the same alphabet substitution code, except more difficult. The Cryptic and Challenger Cryptic Stories require mental discipline and logic; they would be very good for the more advanced child.

"Yankee Doodle"
"The Star-Spangled Banner"
From the Songs of Stephen Foster

1

YANKEE DOODLE

"Yankee Doodle" has a melody whose origin is unknown. Controversial claims come from Ireland, Hungary, Spain, Germany, Holland and England. The verse "Father and I went down to camp . . . ." was thought to have been created at a Colonial soldiers' camp near Cambridge, Massachusetts, during 1775 or 1776. The verse "He stuck a feather in his cap and called it macaroni . . . ." came from the England of Oliver Cromwell's day. This referred to Cromwell going into Oxford riding on a small horse, with a single feather in his hat fastened in a type of knot called a macaroni. The melody was similar to one known by the common people before the 1600's.

NOTABLE TRIVIA

Before and during the Revolutionary War, British soldiers considered "Yankee Doodle" an excellent song. They especially liked British Dr. Richard Shuckburgh's many verses making fun of the Continental Militia. The silent New Englanders decided they liked the melody but didn't care much for the words . . . and made some words of their own. They also made this song their own patriotic field music, marching to it wherever they went.

"YANKEE DOODLE"

OR
"YANKEE . . . WHO?"

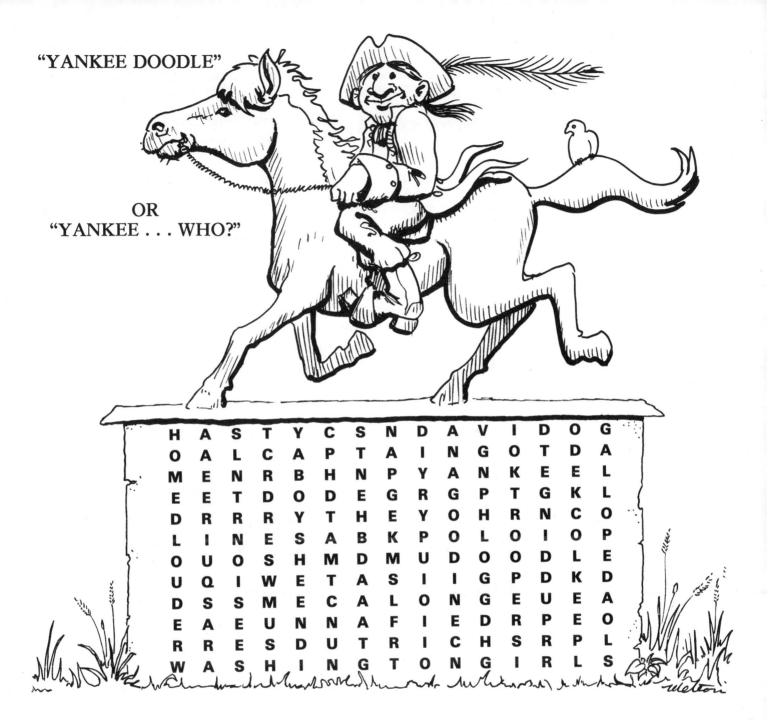

```
H A S T Y C S N D A V I D O G
O A L C A P T A I N G O T D E A
M E N R B H N P Y A N K E E L L
E E T D O D E G R G P T G K C O
D R R R Y T H E Y O H R N I O P
L I N E S A B K P O L O O D L E
O N O S H M D M U D O O D K D
U Q I W E T A S I I G P D K P D
D S S M E C A L O N G E U E A
E A E U N N A F I E D R P E O
R R R S N D U T R I C H S R P L
W A S H I N G T O N G I R L S
```

Yankee Doodle is grinning because he found the Mystery Word that is seven letters long.

WORDS TO FIND

along, boys, camp, captain, cart, dandy, David, day, Doodle, father, galloped, girls, Goodin, got, gun, handy, hasty, head, home, horn, keg, keep, load, locked, log, louder, men, mind, mush, noise, pain, pudding, races, remember, rich, squire, step, they, thousand, troopers, Washington, went, Yankee

3

YANKEE DOODLE

Tie the information together. Social studies and music meet in these facts. Discuss, question and encourage reading and research for deeper understanding of the life of those times.

Yankee Doodle Happenings	During That Time in the United States
1587—Sir Walter Raleigh sent a second group of people to form a colony on Roanoke Island, Virginia.	1587—Common people of England sing a song very similar to the later song "Yankee Doodle."
1774—Colonists are forced to have British soldiers live in their homes.	1774—British soldiers make fun of the Colonial soldiers with derisive words to a song called "Yankee Doodle."
1775—Patrick Henry delivers his speech ending with "Give me liberty or give me death."	1775—Colonial soldiers create their own words to "Yankee Doodle"; it becomes a rallying cry of outrage and patriotism.
1776—British forces have to evacuate Boston.	1776—The British forces begin to dislike the song "Yankee Doodle."
1781—General George Cornwallis surrenders to General George Washington at Yorktown: hostilities cease.	1781—Colonial forces march and sing their own words to "Yankee Doodle" at Yorktown as the British forces lay down their guns in defeat.

TO MAKE THE SUBJECT COME ALIVE
(Suggested Activites for Children)
Yankee Doodle

1. Challenge the children to describe various articles used in George Washington's day (as "Yankee Doodle" described a drum in the song). They must use their own words and things not described in the song.
2. Find different versions of the song. (Originally, it had 14 verses!)
3. Interview a person from England and get his opinion of this song; tell the class about your interview.
4. Have the class sing the song. Add instruments you think would be appropriate . . . such as a drum, etc.
5. See if you can obtain a filmstrip with recording about this song.
6. On George Washington's birthday, or when studying the Revolutionary War, give each child a copy of the Hasty Pudding recipe. The children's parents could help them make it at home.
7. Make Hasty Pudding in the classroom. Let each child choose which of the suggested additions he wants on *his* serving of this food enjoyed so long ago.
8. Learn the minuet . . . the dance Martha and George Washington danced.
9. Discuss how a small boy might feel in a camp of George Washington's soldiers—what he might have seen, felt, smelled, tasted and heard.

NUMBER WORD GAME
Yankee Doodle

Refer to the story section for answers. Place the letters of your answers on the blanks after the clues. Transfer the letters to the same numbered blanks throughout the paragraph below. A story will result.

1. A patriotic song adopted by the American Forces

   " — — — — — — — — — — — — "
       6 3 8 18 11 11   15 13 13 15 12 11

2. The first seven words of the American version

   — — — — — — — — — —
   5 3 1 19 11 7   3 8 15   14

   — — — — — — — — — — — — — —
   9 11 8 1   15 13 9 8   1 13   17 3 10 22

3. Commander in Chief of the American Forces

   — — — — — — — — — — — — — — —
   2 11 13 7 2 11   9 3 16 19 14 8 2 1 13 8

4. Name the town where the British surrendered.

   — — — — — — — —
   6 13 7 18 1 13 9 8

5. Origin of the "Yankee Doodle" melody

   — — — — — — —
   20 8 18 8 13 9 8

6. The colonists made some of their own to a melody they liked.

   — — — — — —
   21 11 7 16 11 16

" — — — — — — — — " — — — — — — — — — — — —
10 3 17 3 7 13 8 14   9 3 16   3   9 13 7 15   9 14 1 19

— — — — — — — — — — — — — — — — — — — — — — — —
16 11 21 11 7 3 12   10 11 3 8 14 8 2 16   14 8   11 8 2 12 3 8 15

— — — — — 1600' —, — — — — — — — — — — — —
13 5   1 19 11   16   14 1   9 3 16   3   18 14 8 15   13 5

— — — — — — — — — — — — — — — — — — — — — —,
18 8 13 1   14 8   7 11 21 13 12 20 1 14 13 8 3 7 6   15 3 6 16

— — — — — — — — — — — — " — — — — — — — —."
14 1   3 12 16 13   10 11 3 8 1   16 1 6 12 14 16 19

5

HASTY PUDDING

This dessert was originally served as porridge.

1 cup yellow cornmeal
1 cup cold water
3 cups water

½ teaspoon salt
Butter or margarine
Maple syrup, brown sugar, molasses, or cream

Combine the cornmeal and cold water. In heavy saucepan bring the 3 cups water and salt to a boil. Carefully stir in the cornmeal mixture, making sure it does not lump. Cook over low heat, stirring occasionally, till mixture is very thick, 10 to 15 minutes. Serve with a pat of butter or margarine, and maple syrup, brown syrup, molasses or cream. Makes 6 or 7 servings.

CRYPTIC STORY
Yankee Doodle

Each story has a message in substitution code. (One letter of the alphabet has been substituted for the correct letter.) When you have discovered one word, use the known letters to help decode other words. Use the clues!

"NCFWP UEHHXQT" ICF C LCRSKXWV LSSH XQ JSYSQXCY CGVKXJCQ NSGVF.

INCWVRVK SQV NCH ICF CHHVH, EFECYYP ZEWWVK, JKVCG SK GXYO. SLWVQ

SQV SL WNV LSYYSIXQT ICF FWXKKVH XQWS WNV LXQXFNVH UEHHXQT:

GSYCFFVF, GCUYV FPKEU, NSQVP SK QEWF.

In this story, the regular letters of the alphabet are represented by other letters. All you have to do is break the code. Here are some hints to give you a start. Good luck! *A* is represented by *C;* *E* by *V;* *N* by *Q;* *D* by *H;* and *I* by *X.*

6

THE STAR-SPANGLED BANNER

''The Star-Spangled Banner'' was adopted as the national anthem of the United States of America in 1931 by an act of Congress. Its creation was the result of a series of events that started in the middle of the night at the end of the summer in 1814, two years after the beginning of the War of 1812. America was at war with England. British soldiers, returning from the Battle of Bladenburg (near Baltimore) forcibly took Dr. William Beanes from his home. He was kept prisoner aboard a British warship. Legend relates that Dr. Beanes treated the ailing sailors, but was not allowed to return to his home. Francis Scott Key, a Baltimore lawyer and friend, located him and persuaded the Admiral to release him; however, they were not allowed to leave just then. The American Fort McHenry protected the entrance of the harbor leading to Baltimore, Maryland . . . and the British wanted to capture the city of Baltimore; the Fort must be captured! Early in the morning of September 13, 1814, the attack started, continuing throughout the day and night until the early hours of September 14. Dr. Beanes and Francis Scott Key watched the bombardment from the deck of the enemy ship. At dawn of September 14, when he saw the American flag, Francis Scott Key completed the poem he had been writing during the night. Upon being released, he showed it to his brother-in-law, who had it published in the newspaper. It was an immediate success!

NOTABLE TRIVIA

The melody used for the poem was frequently heard in taverns of that day. It was a very popular British drinking song!

"THE STAR-SPANGLED BANNER"
OR
"AH . . . OUR FLAG IS STILL THERE!"

```
B  E  A  N  E  S  A  Y  S  P  A  N  G  L  E  D  T  E  V
E  U  T  M  P  R  O  O  F  C  O  N  Q  U  E  R  K  I  E
A  K  R  A  I  N  S  R  A  T  S  P  E  S  U  A  C  L  A
M  L  O  N  G  S  A  D  G  N  I  E  E  S  W  T  B  B  R
A  A  F  M  E  N  T  N  L  L  A  S  T  A  O  A  A  E  L
S  T  D  P  C  D  I  D  U  A  E  N  T  R  C  L  O  T  Y
T  T  I  A  H  N  B  O  T  R  C  Y  R  T  E  T  W  E  R
E  O  S  W  A  E  D  M  C  B  I  N  I  A  S  T  E  R  O
K  C  N  A  L  O  L  N  E  O  T  R  M  E  W  P  O  E  H
C  S  W  G  L  A  N  D  R  M  B  O  A  D  L  A  M  N  S
O  E  N  L  A  W  Y  E  R  Y  R  S  R  V  A  I  V  A  R
R  E  P  O  S  E  S  A  F  E  R  A  L  G  E  S  S  E  R
```

The nine-letter Mystery Word is what the American soldiers proved to be.

WORDS TO FIND

able, admiral, armed, awake, Baltimore, beam, Beanes, between, bombing, brave, burned, cause, conquer, dawns, doctor, early, England, fort, Francis, glare, land, last, lawyer, Madison, McHenry, mist, motto, peace, proof, rain, ramparts, reposes, rockets, safer, say, Scott, seeing, Sept., shore, silence, spangled, stars, tales, talk, trust, victory, Washington, wave

THE STAR-SPANGLED BANNER

Tie the information together. Social studies and music meet in these facts. Discuss, question and encourage reading and research for deeper understanding of the life of those times.

Happenings Concerning This Song

1814, Midsummer— Dr. Beanes taken from his home by British soldiers.

1814, September 12—Francis Scott Key talks British Admiral into releasing Dr. Beanes . . . "but not right now"

1814, September 13-14—British Navy attacks Fort McHenry; Key and Dr. Beanes watch from the deck of a British warship.

1814, September 15—Dr. Beanes and Francis Scott Key released by the British Admiral. The attack on Fort McHenry has failed.

1814, September 16—A broadsheet containing the poem by Francis Scott Key is published . . . it is an immediate success.

During That Time . in the United States

1814—For the second year, lead pencils are manufactured in Concord, Massachusetts.

1814—British soldiers burn the White House and the Capitol in Washington, D.C.

1814—At Harvard College in Cambridge, Massachusetts, the cost of attending for one year is $300.

1814—The first factory for processing cotton into cloth is opened in Massachusetts.

MAKING THE SUBJECT COME ALIVE
(Suggested Activities for Children)
The Star-Spangled Banner

1. Describe (or dramatize) a conversation between Dr. Beanes and the British soldiers when he is forcibly taken from his home.
2. Act out how Francis Scott Key and Dr. Beanes reacted during the attack on Fort McHenry (a) when the attack started (b) in the middle of the night during the height of the attack (c) at dawn when all was silent and they saw somebody's flag flying, but the mist prevented them from seeing whose flag it was.
3. Imagine how Francis Scott Key and Dr. Beanes expressed their feelings and how they coped with ordinary things (a) Did they get hungry? (b) What did they eat? (c) Were they fed by the enemy sailors? (d) Did they sit down on chairs? (e) Did they get cold during that long night? How did they get warm? (f) Francis Scott Key expressed some of his emotions by writing the poem on an old envelope. How did Dr. Beanes express his emotions—sharpen his instruments, count his pills, practice bandaging, count the stars?
4. Write to the Chamber of Commerce in Baltimore, Maryland, and ask for information about Fort McHenry and the way it is today.
5. Make a tape recording of your class singing "The Star-Spangled Banner," and play it over the intercom of your school for all to sing and enjoy.

NUMBER WORD GAME
The Star-Spangled Banner

Refer to the story section for answers. Place the letters of your answers on the blanks after the clues. Transfer the letters to the same numbered blanks throughout the paragraph below. A story will result.

1. What is the name of the kindly medical doctor?

    $\overline{3}\ \overline{1}.\quad \overline{22}\ \overline{5}\ \overline{13}\ \overline{6}\ \overline{5}\ \overline{4}$

2. During what war did this adventure occur?

    $\overline{14}\ \overline{13}\ \overline{1}\quad \overline{10}\ \overline{7}\quad 1812$

3. Name the month when Fort McHenry was attacked.

    $\overline{4}\ \overline{5}\ \overline{23}\ \overline{8}\ \overline{5}\ \overline{2}\ \overline{22}\ \overline{5}\ \overline{1}$

4. What is the name of the lawyer who wrote the poem "The Star-Spangled Banner"?

    $\overline{7}\ \overline{1}\ \overline{13}\ \overline{6}\ \overline{11}\ \overline{18}\ \overline{4}\quad \overline{4}\ \overline{11}\ \overline{10}\ \overline{8}\ \overline{8}\quad \overline{12}\ \overline{5}\ \overline{17}$

5. This is the national anthem of what country?

    $\overline{21}\ \overline{6}\ \overline{18}\ \overline{8}\ \overline{5}\ \overline{3}\quad \overline{4}\ \overline{8}\ \overline{13}\ \overline{8}\ \overline{5}\ \overline{4}$

    $\overline{10}\ \overline{7}\quad \overline{13}\ \overline{2}\ \overline{5}\ \overline{1}\ \overline{18}\ \overline{11}\ \overline{13}$

6. Write the last five words of verse one.

    $\overline{8}\ \overline{15}\ \overline{5}\quad \overline{15}\ \overline{10}\ \overline{2}\ \overline{5}\quad \overline{10}\ \overline{7}$

    $\overline{8}\ \overline{15}\ \overline{5}\quad \overline{22}\ \overline{1}\ \overline{13}\ \overline{9}\ \overline{5}$

7. How did Dr. Beanes and Francis Scott Key feel when allowed to go home?

    $\overline{20}\ \overline{19}\ \overline{13}\ \overline{3}$

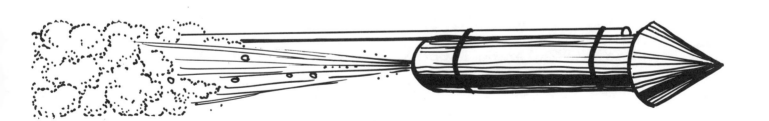

$\overline{3}\ \overline{5}\ \overline{4}\ \overline{11}\ \overline{5}\ \overline{6}\ \overline{3}\ \overline{13}\ \overline{6}\ \overline{8}\ \overline{4}\quad \overline{10}\ \overline{7}\quad \overline{7}\ \overline{1}\ \overline{13}\ \overline{6}\ \overline{11}\ \overline{18}\ \overline{4}$

$\overline{4}\ \overline{11}\ \overline{10}\ \overline{8}\ \overline{8}\quad \overline{12}\ \overline{5}\ \overline{17}\quad \overline{13}\ \overline{1}\ \overline{5}\quad \overline{19}\ \overline{18}\ \overline{9}\ \overline{18}\ \overline{6}\ \overline{20}\quad \overline{8}\ \overline{10}\ \overline{3}\ \overline{13}\ \overline{17}$

$\overline{18}\ \overline{6}\quad \overline{9}\ \overline{13}\ \overline{1}\ \overline{18}\ \overline{10}\ \overline{21}\ \overline{4}\quad \overline{4}\ \overline{8}\ \overline{13}\ \overline{8}\ \overline{5}\ \overline{4}\quad \overline{10}\ \overline{7}\quad \overline{10}\ \overline{21}\ \overline{1}$

$\overline{14}\ \overline{10}\ \overline{6}\ \overline{3}\ \overline{5}\ \overline{1}\ \overline{7}\ \overline{21}\ \overline{19}\quad \overline{11}\ \overline{10}\ \overline{21}\ \overline{6}\ \overline{8}\ \overline{1}\ \overline{17}.$

11

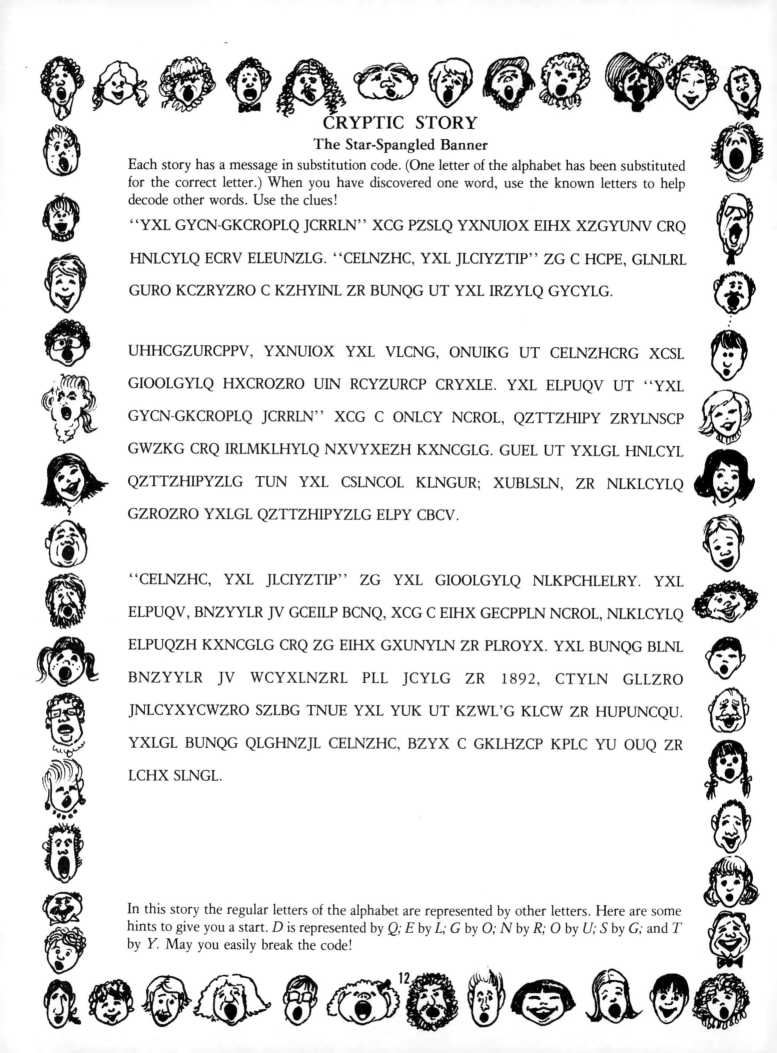

CRYPTIC STORY
The Star-Spangled Banner

Each story has a message in substitution code. (One letter of the alphabet has been substituted for the correct letter.) When you have discovered one word, use the known letters to help decode other words. Use the clues!

"YXL GYCN-GKCROPLQ JCRRLN" XCG PZSLQ YXNUIOX EIHX XZGYUNV CRQ HNLCYLQ ECRV ELEUNZLG. "CELNZHC, YXL JLCIYZTIP" ZG C HCPE, GLNLRL GURO KCZRYZRO C KZHYINL ZR BUNQG UT YXL IRZYLQ GYCYLG.

UHHCGZURCPPV, YXNUIOX YXL VLCNG, ONUIKG UT CELNZHCRG XCSL GIOOLGYLQ HXCROZRO UIN RCYZURCP CRYXLE. YXL ELPUQV UT "YXL GYCN-GKCROPLQ JCRRLN" XCG C ONLCY NCROL, QZTTZHIPY ZRYLNSCP GWZKG CRQ IRLMKLHYLQ NXVYXEZH KXNCGLG. GUEL UT YXLGL HNLCYL QZTTZHIPYZLG TUN YXL CSLNCOL KLNGUR; XUBLSLN, ZR NLKLCYLQ GZROZRO YXLGL QZTTZHIPYZLG ELPY CBCV.

"CELNZHC, YXL JLCIYZTIP" ZG YXL GIOOLGYLQ NLKPCHLELRY. YXL ELPUQV, BNZYYLR JV GCEILP BCNQ, XCG C EIHX GECPPLN NCROL, NLKLCYLQ ELPUQZH KXNCGLG CRQ ZG EIHX GXUNYLN ZR PLROYX. YXL BUNQG BLNL BNZYYLR JV WCYXLNZRL PLL JCYLG ZR 1892, CTYLN GLLZRO JNLCYXYCWZRO SZLBG TNUE YXL YUK UT KZWL'G KLCW ZR HUPUNCQU. YXLGL BUNQG QLGHNZJL CELNZHC, BZYX C GKLHZCP KPLC YU OUQ ZR LCHX SLNGL.

In this story the regular letters of the alphabet are represented by other letters. Here are some hints to give you a start. *D* is represented by *Q; E* by *L; G* by *O; N* by *R; O* by *U; S* by *G;* and *T* by *Y.* May you easily break the code!

12

FROM THE SONGS OF STEPHEN FOSTER

The songs of Stephen Foster reflect his love of home, family and friends. Melodically, his songs are simple, short and have a catchy "toe tapping" quality. They reflect emotions common to everyone and possess the simplicity of a folk song. People took his songs to their hearts and made them their own. "Oh! Susanna" became the favorite of the "Young 49'ers"; "My Old Kentucky Home" became the state song of Kentucky.

Stephen Collins Foster was born on July 4, 1826, in Lawrenceville, Pennsylvania, then a suburb of Pittsburgh. In 1850 he married Jane McDowell; they had one daughter. Life was not easy for this dreamer and creator of heart-warming songs. He died, penniless and alone in New York City in January, 1864.

NOTABLE TRIVIA

Stephen and his brother had a problem finding the name of a river that would fit the song. Finally, they searched an atlas and found the name of Swanee River, located in northern Florida.

FROM THE SONGS OF STEPHEN FOSTER
OR
"TOE TAPPING . . . HEART TOUCHING"

```
S U S A N N A H A T C R M H
W O R A I N O A T E A R A O O
A L J G L R M A N C M P O M E
N D H N S D E W E E P A R Y F
E T G E A H R T L Y T R Y F E
E O S S W B R R L E O E L O L
D A H K A A Y U Y E W V U L K
N B C Y C A K E A N N I J K
E U M K E N T U C K Y R D S
B O B T A I L A S E I D A L
```

The seven-letter Mystery Word is a place mentioned in one of Stephen Foster's songs.

WORDS TO FIND

banjo, bay, bend, bobtail, buckwheat, cake, Camptown, dah, dog, dry, folks, happy, hat, home, horses, July, Kentucky, knee, ladies, old, merry, Nelly, night, racetrack, rain, river, roam, sad, Susanna, Swanee, tear, true, weep

15

From the Songs of Stephen Foster

Tie the information together. Social studies and music meet in these facts. Discuss, question and encourage reading and research for deeper understanding of the life of those times.

Happenings Concerning Stephen Foster's Songs

1826—Stephen Collins Foster was born on July 4, in Lawrenceville, Pennsylvania.

1840—Stephen Foster composes his first piece, a waltz for four flutes.

1848—"Oh! Susanna" is composed by Stephen Foster.

1849—The "Young 49'ers" make "Oh! Susanna" their theme song as they travel to California.

1850—Stephen Foster marries Jane McDowell.

1853—Foster composes "My Old Kentucky Home."

1864—In January, Stephen Collins Foster dies in New York City.

During That Time in the United States

1826—*The Last of the Mohicans,* a frontier story by James Fenimore Cooper, is published.

1840—William Henry Harrison is elected President.

1848—Wisconsin becomes the 30th state.

1849—The giant redwood trees in California are given the name of sequoias, in honor of Cherokee Indian chief and educator, Sequoya.

1850—For the first time, mail is carried from Independence, Missouri, to Salt Lake City, Utah, once a month.

1853—For the first time, the railroad is established from Chicago, Illinois, to eastern cities.

1864—Nevada becomes the 36th state.

MAKING THE SUBJECT COME ALIVE
(Suggested Activities for Children)
From the Songs of Stephen Foster

1. Imagine a conversation between Stephen and his brother as they try to decide the name of a river in the song "Old Folks at Home." This could be comical as they try various names, trying to find one with the correct number of syllables, yet is still a real river.
2. Write to the Chamber of Commerce in Pittsburgh, Pennsylvania, and request information about Stephen Foster, his original home, his descendants, etc. They will probably send you some brochures.
3. Organize your own chorus and sing a group of Stephen Foster songs.
4. Write to Bardstown, Kentucky, Chamber of Commerce for information about the annual musical about Stephen Foster and about the mansion where he is said to have composed "My Old Kentucky Home."

NUMBER WORD GAME
From the Songs of Stephen Foster

Refer to the story section for answers. Place the letters of your answers on the blanks after the clues. Transfer the letters to the same numbered blanks throughout the paragraph below. A story will result.

1. Name the city and state where Stephen Foster was born.

    $\overline{1}$ $\overline{5}$ $\overline{4}$ $\overline{11}$ $\overline{15}$ $\overline{3}$ $\overline{20}$ $\overline{15}$ $\overline{21}$ $\overline{16}$ $\overline{1}$ $\overline{1}$ $\overline{15}$,

    $\overline{22}$ $\overline{15}$ $\overline{3}$ $\overline{3}$ $\overline{24}$ $\overline{17}$ $\overline{1}$ $\overline{21}$ $\overline{5}$ $\overline{3}$ $\overline{16}$ $\overline{5}$

2. Name the theme song of the "Young 49'ers."

    " $\overline{8}$ $\overline{13}$! $\overline{24}$ $\overline{14}$ $\overline{24}$ $\overline{5}$ $\overline{3}$ $\overline{3}$ $\overline{5}$ "

3. Name the location of the home that inspired "My Old Kentucky Home."

    $\overline{7}$ $\overline{5}$ $\overline{11}$ $\overline{12}$ $\overline{24}$ $\overline{19}$ $\overline{8}$ $\overline{4}$ $\overline{3}$, $\overline{9}$ $\overline{15}$ $\overline{3}$ $\overline{19}$ $\overline{14}$ $\overline{20}$ $\overline{9}$ $\overline{17}$

4. This composer's full name

    $\overline{24}$ $\overline{19}$ $\overline{15}$ $\overline{22}$ $\overline{13}$ $\overline{15}$ $\overline{3}$ $\quad$ $\overline{20}$ $\overline{8}$ $\overline{1}$ $\overline{1}$ $\overline{16}$ $\overline{3}$ $\overline{24}$

    $\overline{23}$ $\overline{8}$ $\overline{24}$ $\overline{19}$ $\overline{15}$ $\overline{11}$

5. Two things his songs reflected

    $\overline{1}$ $\overline{8}$ $\overline{21}$ $\overline{15}$ $\quad$ $\overline{8}$ $\overline{23}$ $\quad$ $\overline{13}$ $\overline{8}$ $\overline{18}$ $\overline{15}$ $\quad$ $\overline{5}$ $\overline{3}$ $\overline{12}$

    $\overline{23}$ $\overline{5}$ $\overline{18}$ $\overline{16}$ $\overline{1}$ $\overline{17}$

$\overline{19}$ $\overline{13}$ $\overline{15}$ $\quad$ $\overline{8}$ $\overline{1}$ $\overline{12}$ $\quad$ $\overline{11}$ $\overline{8}$ $\overline{4}$ $\overline{5}$ $\overline{3}$ $\quad$ $\overline{13}$ $\overline{8}$ $\overline{18}$ $\overline{15}$ $\quad$ $\overline{16}$ $\overline{3}$

$\overline{7}$ $\overline{5}$ $\overline{11}$ $\overline{12}$ $\overline{24}$ $\overline{19}$ $\overline{8}$ $\overline{4}$ $\overline{3}$, $\overline{9}$ $\overline{15}$ $\overline{3}$ $\overline{19}$ $\overline{14}$ $\overline{20}$ $\overline{9}$ $\overline{17}$ $\quad$ $\overline{16}$ $\overline{24}$ $\quad$ $\overline{4}$ $\overline{13}$ $\overline{15}$ $\overline{11}$ $\overline{15}$

$\overline{24}$ $\overline{19}$ $\overline{15}$ $\overline{22}$ $\overline{13}$ $\overline{15}$ $\overline{3}$ $\quad$ $\overline{20}$ $\overline{8}$ $\overline{1}$ $\overline{1}$ $\overline{16}$ $\overline{3}$ $\overline{24}$ $\quad$ $\overline{23}$ $\overline{8}$ $\overline{24}$ $\overline{19}$ $\overline{15}$ $\overline{11}$

$\overline{21}$ $\overline{16}$ $\overline{24}$ $\overline{16}$ $\overline{19}$ $\overline{15}$ $\overline{12}$ $\quad$ $\overline{13}$ $\overline{16}$ $\overline{24}$ $\quad$ $\overline{20}$ $\overline{8}$ $\overline{14}$ $\overline{24}$ $\overline{16}$ $\overline{3}$ $\overline{24}$. $\quad$ $\overline{1}$ $\overline{15}$ $\overline{10}$ $\overline{15}$ $\overline{3}$ $\overline{12}$

$\overline{24}$ $\overline{5}$ $\overline{17}$ $\overline{24}$ $\quad$ " $\overline{18}$ $\overline{17}$ $\quad$ $\overline{8}$ $\overline{1}$ $\overline{12}$ $\quad$ $\overline{9}$ $\overline{15}$ $\overline{3}$ $\overline{19}$ $\overline{14}$ $\overline{20}$ $\overline{9}$ $\overline{17}$ $\quad$ $\overline{13}$ $\overline{8}$ $\overline{18}$ $\overline{15}$ "

$\overline{4}$ $\overline{5}$ $\overline{24}$ $\quad$ $\overline{4}$ $\overline{11}$ $\overline{16}$ $\overline{19}$ $\overline{19}$ $\overline{15}$ $\overline{3}$ $\quad$ $\overline{13}$ $\overline{15}$ $\overline{11}$ $\overline{15}$ $\quad$ $\overline{16}$ $\overline{3}$ $\quad$ 1853.

17

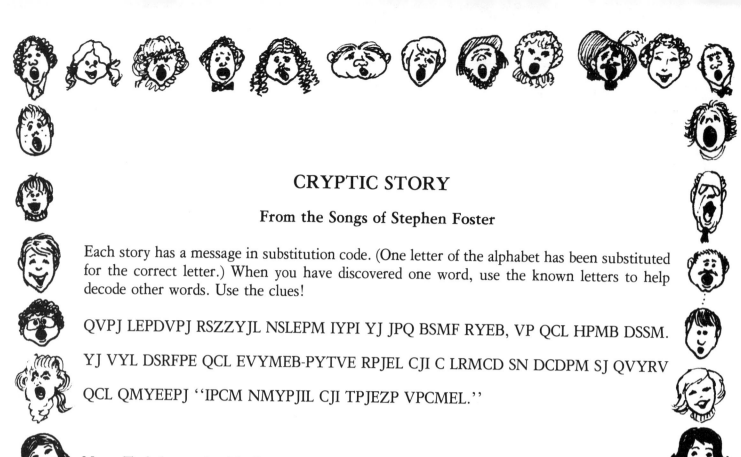

CRYPTIC STORY

From the Songs of Stephen Foster

Each story has a message in substitution code. (One letter of the alphabet has been substituted for the correct letter.) When you have discovered one word, use the known letters to help decode other words. Use the clues!

QVPJ LEPDVPJ RSZZYJL NSLEPM IYPI YJ JPQ BSMF RYEB, VP QCL HPMB DSSM.

YJ VYL DSRFPE QCL EVYMEB-PYTVE RPJEL CJI C LRMCD SN DCDPM SJ QVYRV

QCL QMYEEPJ "IPCM NMYPJIL CJI TPJEZP VPCMEL."

Note: To help you in this Cryptic Story, here are some letters and what they represent. *A* is represented by *C; E* by *P; N* by *J; D* by *I; R* by *M.* Good luck in breaking the code!

CHALLENGER CRYPTIC STORY

KRTKCR IRBR ERCRJBFGZSO RMRBAIDRBR. . . ZG IFX GDR HTYBGD TH UYCA,

1826. HZHGA ARFBX FOT TS GDZX VFA, GDR VRECFBFGZTS TH

ZSVRKRSVRSER DFV JRRS XZOSRV. XFVCA, GIT KFGBZTGX IDT DRCKRV GT

EBRFGR GDZX VTEYQRSG VZRV TS GDZX MRBA VFA, UTDS FVFQX FSV GDT-

QFX URHHRBXTS. TS GDZX VFA TH DFKKZSRXX FSV OBZRH, XGRKDRS ETC-

CZSX HTXGRB IFX JTBS.

Here are some clues to get you started on this more difficult cryptic story . . . a challenger. *A* is represented by *F; E* by *R; F* by *H;* and *T* by *G.* Good luck!

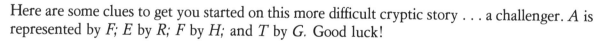

George Frideric Handel
Franz Schubert
Giuseppe Verdi
Peter Ilich Tchaikovsky
John Philip Sousa
Sergei Prokofiev

GEORGE FRIDERIC HANDEL

George Frideric Handel was born on February 23, 1685, in Halle, (HAHL-LUH) Germany. As a child he showed musical talent and at an early age was quite an outstanding organist and harpsichordist.

When he was nineteen years old, he was fortunate to hear one of the world's greatest organists and composers of that time, Dietrich Buxtehude. In 1707, he visited Rome and stayed in Italy for three years, becoming thoroughly indoctrinated in the technique of Italian opera. Several operas were composed using that style. When financial returns from the operas were not profitable, he turned to oratorios. It was in this field he left an indelible mark.

At the age of 56, struggling against ill health, debt and almost friendless, his valiant spirit gave him courage and he created his most famous oratorio, *Messiah.* It was first presented in Dublin, Ireland, and was a rousing success. In England, acceptance was slower; four to six years passed before performances took place.

How he loved food . . . little restraint was used when it came to eating! It certainly showed, for he was very large, on the fat side one might say; he moved in a rather clumsy manner. His smile and laughter were delightful; however, when a scowl or frown appeared on his face, beware. Many stories are told about his violent temper and how he dealt with temperamental musicians and producers.

''Borrowing'' (actually *taking)* melodies from other musicians was the practice of the day; everyone did it. However, Handel ''borrowed'' more than most composers. Defending himself, he remarked, ''They (other composers) don't know what to do with those tunes, and I do.'' He gave added life, lustre and beauty to melodies that previously seemed lifeless. Today, copyright laws prohibit such ''borrowing.''

Handel belongs to the music period classified as baroque, which was characterized by very elaborate and almost theatrical style.

The last eight years of his life were lived in darkness, for he was blind. Queen Anne of England gave him a lifelong pension. He died on Good Friday, 1759. England's respect for him was evident by having him buried in the Poet's Corner of Westminster Abbey.

NOTABLE TRIVIA

At the first performance of the oratorio, *Messiah*, men were asked not to wear their swords. Women were requested not to wear hoops. This made room for one hundred more seats!

GEORGE FRIDERIC HANDEL
OR
"BORROWING GEORGE"

WORDS TO FIND
Almira, barge, blind, borrowing, Buxtehude, debt, Dublin, duel, eight, England, gain, Germany, Halle, hallelujah, Hamburg, hit, largo, London, meet, melody, *Messiah,* mood, opera, organ, oratorios, play, rage, Rome, St. John, Thames, Xerxes

```
B U X T E H U D E H R A G E N
A O E S G E R M A N Y S N I O
R G R A O S T J O H N G L M D
G R X R C I U D N I L B E E N
E A E S O L R R R A U S U E O
E L S P E W O O N D S N D T L
L E E L P M I D T I I A E H D
L R L D E L A N A A H G B G O
A A L M I R A H G I R R T I O
H A M B U R G Y T Y D O L E M
```

The six-letter Mystery Word indicates the type of music he composed most frequently.

22

GEORGE FRIDERIC HANDEL

Tie the information together. Social studies and music meet in these facts. Discuss, question and encourage reading and research for deeper understanding of the life of those times.

Happenings in His Life

1685—George Frideric Handel was born on February 23, 1685, in Halle, Germany.

1703—George Frideric leaves Halle to study in Hamburg, Germany.

1704—Handel heard the Danish organist, Buxtehude in Lubeck. Handel was 19 years old.

1741—Handel wrote the oratorio *Messiah.*

1752—Handel becomes blind.

1759—Handel dies on Good Friday, April 14, 1759.

During That Time in the United States

1685—La Salle leads a French expedition that explores East Texas.

1685—William Bradford set up a printing press in Philadelphia.

1703—In Charleston, South Carolina, the first professional actors perform.

1704—Men, women and children were killed by French and Indians in the town of Deerfield, Massachusetts.

1741—Alaska is discovered by a Danish explorer in the service of Russia.

1742—*Messiah* is performed in Bethlehem, Pennsylvania.

1752—Benjamin Franklin and his famous kite prove that lightning is electricity.

1759—Shipbuilders in the colonies made almost 400 ships each year.

MAKING THE SUBJECT COME ALIVE
(Suggested Activities for Children)
George Frideric Handel

1. After a discussion on the subject, let two children use their wits and imagination. Have one child be Handel and the other a composer whose music Handel has "borrowed" . . . who demands his rights and wants his melody back.
2. Pretend you are Handel writing a letter to your boss, who happens to be a King. You are asking for a month's leave of absence to go to England.
3. Discover why everyone stands when the "Hallelujah" chorus from the *Messiah* is sung.
4. Listen to some of Handel's music . . . discover which of his compositions you like . . . or dislike. Always be able to give a reason why you do or don't like a composition.
5. Imagine you are the manager of the new music hall on Fishamble Street in Dublin where the *Messiah* is to be presented. Pretend to figure how much space a sword and a hoop skirt would take, since they are forbidden during this first performance. See how many more chairs can be used.

NUMBER WORD GAME
George Frideric Handel

Refer to the story section for answers. Place the letters of your answers on the blanks after the clues. Transfer the letters to the same numbered blanks throughout the paragraph below. A story will result.

1. A famous organist Handel heard as a youth

$\overline{8}$ $\overline{9}$ $\overline{7}$ $\overline{3}$ $\overline{14}$ $\overline{5}$ $\overline{9}$ $\overline{16}$ $\overline{14}$

2. What gave Handel great delight three times a day?

$\overline{12}$ $\overline{1}$ $\overline{1}$ $\overline{16}$

3. One of his best loved oratorios

" $\overline{2}$ $\overline{14}$ $\overline{15}$ $\overline{15}$ $\overline{17}$ $\overline{4}$ $\overline{5}$ "

4. This trait of his caused great consternation.

$\overline{21}$ $\overline{17}$ $\overline{1}$ $\overline{18}$ $\overline{14}$ $\overline{13}$ $\overline{3}$ $\overline{3}$ $\overline{14}$ $\overline{2}$ $\overline{19}$ $\overline{14}$ $\overline{10}$

5. This composer's first name

$\overline{22}$ $\overline{14}$ $\overline{1}$ $\overline{10}$ $\overline{22}$ $\overline{14}$

6. Where is he buried?

$\overline{19}$ $\overline{1}$ $\overline{14}$ $\overline{3}$ $\overline{15}$ $\overline{20}$ $\overline{1}$ $\overline{10}$ $\overline{13}$ $\overline{14}$ $\overline{10}$ $\overline{17}$ $\overline{13}$

$\overline{6}$ $\overline{14}$ $\overline{15}$ $\overline{3}$ $\overline{2}$ $\overline{17}$ $\overline{13}$ $\overline{15}$ $\overline{3}$ $\overline{14}$ $\overline{10}$ $\overline{4}$ $\overline{8}$ $\overline{8}$ $\overline{14}$ $\overline{11}$

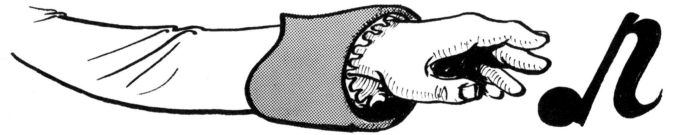

$\overline{5}$ $\overline{4}$ $\overline{13}$ $\overline{16}$ $\overline{14}$ $\overline{18}$ $\overline{15}$, $\overline{1}$ $\overline{10}$ $\overline{4}$ $\overline{3}$ $\overline{1}$ $\overline{10}$ $\overline{17}$ $\overline{1}$

" $\overline{2}$ $\overline{14}$ $\overline{15}$ $\overline{15}$ $\overline{17}$ $\overline{4}$ $\overline{5}$ " $\overline{6}$ $\overline{4}$ $\overline{15}$ $\overline{20}$ $\overline{1}$ $\overline{2}$ $\overline{19}$ $\overline{1}$ $\overline{15}$ $\overline{14}$ $\overline{16}$ $\overline{21}$ $\overline{14}$ $\overline{10}$ $\overline{11}$

$\overline{10}$ $\overline{4}$ $\overline{19}$ $\overline{17}$ $\overline{16}$ $\overline{18}$ $\overline{11}$. $\overline{1}$ $\overline{13}$ $\overline{14}$ $\overline{15}$ $\overline{4}$ $\overline{3}$ $\overline{9}$ $\overline{10}$ $\overline{16}$ $\overline{4}$ $\overline{11}$ $\overline{5}$ $\overline{14}$

$\overline{15}$ $\overline{3}$ $\overline{4}$ $\overline{10}$ $\overline{3}$ $\overline{14}$ $\overline{16}$ $\overline{6}$ $\overline{10}$ $\overline{17}$ $\overline{3}$ $\overline{17}$ $\overline{13}$ $\overline{22}$. $\overline{17}$ $\overline{3}$ $\overline{6}$ $\overline{4}$ $\overline{15}$

$\overline{4}$ $\overline{9}$ $\overline{22}$ $\overline{9}$ $\overline{15}$ $\overline{3}$ 22, 1741. $\overline{3}$ $\overline{6}$ $\overline{14}$ $\overline{13}$ $\overline{3}$ $\overline{11}$ $\overline{12}$ $\overline{1}$ $\overline{9}$ $\overline{10}$ - $\overline{16}$ $\overline{4}$ $\overline{11}$ $\overline{15}$

$\overline{18}$ $\overline{4}$ $\overline{3}$ $\overline{14}$ $\overline{10}$ $\overline{1}$ $\overline{13}$ $\overline{15}$ $\overline{14}$ $\overline{19}$ $\overline{3}$ $\overline{14}$ $\overline{2}$ $\overline{8}$ $\overline{14}$ $\overline{10}$ 14, 1741, $\overline{17}$ $\overline{3}$

$\overline{6}$ $\overline{4}$ $\overline{15}$ $\overline{20}$ $\overline{1}$ $\overline{2}$ $\overline{19}$ $\overline{18}$ $\overline{14}$ $\overline{3}$ $\overline{14}$ $\overline{16}$.

CRYPTIC STORY
George Frideric Handel

Each story has a message in substitution code. (One letter of the alphabet has been substituted for the correct letter.) When you have discovered one word, use the known letters to help decode other words. Use the clues!

SDEOKW RDX FDWWKO HSK ''XSDZKXTKDUK JL QYXNF'' PI ZNEV VKJUVK

111 JL KEVWDEO. HSK ZNEV TWDIKO HSK SDUTXNFSJUO, GNJWNE DEO

LWYHK DEO WNZKO HJ TWDI SDEOKW'X QYXNF JE HSKXK NEXHUYQKEHX.

RSKEKGKU D FJEFKUH RDX TUKXKEHKO DH HSK TDWDFK, SK NEXNXHKO

HSDH XJQK JL SDEOKW'X QYXNF PK JE HSK TUJVUDQ.

Here are some helps to start you off with this story about Handel. *A* is represented by *D; E* by *K; L* by *W; N* by *E; T* by *H* and *R* by *U.* May you enjoy being a detective as you solve this story!

CHALLENGER CRYPTIC STORY

ONQA NFAJQT OSKHQJ, NQ SPCQA ZSACYARQJ CNKSRDN CNQ JFM FAJ

AYDNC. YJQFV VQQXQJ CS ZSACYARSRVTM PTSO OYCN QFVQ. ONQA PSSJ

OFV LKSRDNC PSK NYX, YC KQXFYAQJ RANQQJQJ. NYV FLYTYCM CS OSKH

OFV FXFGYAD.

In this story about Handel, here are some helps to start you off. *A* is represented by *F, E* by *Q; N* by *A; T* by *C; O* by *S* and *H* by *N.*

FRANZ SCHUBERT

Franz Peter Schubert was born on January 31, 1797, in the village of Lichtental, then a suburb of Vienna. He was the twelfth of fourteen children born to the village schoolmaster and his wife.

As a young boy, his clear, true voice earned him a scholarship to the Konviktschule in Vienna. This was the choir school for boys who would sing in the Royal Court Chapel. It started him on the path of music. At the age of eleven, he had developed into a good pianist and violinist as well as a composer. During the year he was 18 years old he wrote over 600 songs! His treatment of the art song (*lied* in German) lifted it to new heights. In the art song, the melody follows the words of the poem. Schubert made the accompaniment soar in creating descriptive moods reflected from the words. Composers of this Romantic period of music expressed emotion in their music; a particular mood or feeling was very important.

Franz Schubert was only five feet, one and one-half inches tall and was inclined to be plump. His friends called him ''Tubby'' or ''Schwammer'' in German . . . literally meaning ''Little Mushroom.''

Among his many musical gifts was the ability to create beautiful, flowing melodies. They seemed to flow from his pen with great ease; he also composed extremely fast. One day he met some friends at a village inn. A book of Shakespeare's works happened to fall on the floor. As he reached to pick it up, his eyes lit on the words, ''Hark, Hark, the Lark.'' Immediately musical ideas began to race and flow. Some say he wrote the beautiful song on a menu; others say it was written on a tablecloth. Whichever it was, the world was given a glorious song.

In addition to writing art songs, he wrote in many other fields. He wrote eight symphonies; the *Unfinished* is loved the world over. Operas, operettas, choral works, piano words, and some outstanding string quartets and quintets . . . all were written with the charm and recognizable melodic quality of Schubert.

He greatly admired Ludwig van Beethoven. The admiration was evidently returned, for Beethoven asked to see Schubert during his last illness . . . one of the few people he wanted to visit him. Franz Schubert was one of the torchbearers at Beethoven's funeral.

Almost a year later, on November 19, 1828, the world lost this great giver of melodies; he died of typhoid fever. He was only thirty-one years old.

NOTABLE TRIVIA

During his last illness, Schubert read James Fenimore Cooper's novels in a German edition.

FRANZ SCHUBERT   OR   "THE SHY VIENNESE MUSICIAN"

The six-letter Mystery Word is one of the musical
gifts Schubert possessed.

WORDS TO FIND

ave, choirboy, compose, creative, ease, "Erlking," fee, genius, hark, lied, menu,
Salzburg, serenade, symphony, thirty-one, tragic, Vienna, voice

FRANZ SCHUBERT

Tie the information together! Social studies and music meet in these facts. Discuss, question and encourage reading and research for deeper understanding of the life of those times.

Happenings in His Life	During That Time in the United States
1797—Franz Schubert is born on January 31, 1797, in Lichtental, Austria.	1797—John Adams is elected President.
1809—Vienna is bombed by the French. Franz is 12 years old and experiences this attack.	1809—Illinois Territory is formed from the western part of Indiana Territory.
1815—This year Franz composes 145 songs. He is 18 years old.	1814—British soldiers burn the capital and the White House.
1827—Ludwig van Beethoven dies; Franz Schubert is a torchbearer at his funeral.	1827—Audubon publishes his pictures of *Birds of America.*
1828—Franz Schubert dies on November 19.	1828—Andrew Jackson is elected President.

MAKING THE SUBJECT COME ALIVE
(Suggested Activities for Children)
Franz Schubert

1. Make your own map of Austria. Locate Vienna on your map.
2. Read about life in Vienna at the time Schubert was living there. Decide whether or not you would have liked to be there at that time; be sure to give reason for your decision.
3. Be an eyeglass salesman. Try to sell Schubert a pair of ''Never-Get-Lost'' glasses. (He often seemed to misplace his glasses.)
4. Pretend to be a piano tuner. Carry on a conversation with Schubert about any of his compositions that you know. Be sure to charge an exorbitant amount of money for your tuning. Imagine what his reaction and remarks might have been (he never did have very much money) . . . or do not charge any money at all, for he has given the world so much enjoyment.

NUMBER WORD GAME
Franz Peter Schubert

Refer to the story section for answers. Place the letters of your answers on the blanks after the clues. Transfer the letters to the same numbered blanks throughout the paragraph below. A story will result.

1. Give the complete name of this com- poser.
   $\underline{\hphantom{x}}\ \underline{\hphantom{x}}\ \underline{\hphantom{x}}\ \underline{\hphantom{x}}\ \underline{\hphantom{x}}\quad \underline{\hphantom{x}}\ \underline{\hphantom{x}}\ \underline{\hphantom{x}}\ \underline{\hphantom{x}}\ \underline{\hphantom{x}}\quad \underline{\hphantom{x}}\ \underline{\hphantom{x}}\ \underline{\hphantom{x}}\ \underline{\hphantom{x}}\ \underline{\hphantom{x}}\ \underline{\hphantom{x}}\ \underline{\hphantom{x}}$
   2 13 9 12 6   3 4 5 4 13   20 16 10 23 17 4 13 5

2. Name the month when he was born.
   $\underline{\hphantom{x}}\ \underline{\hphantom{x}}\ \underline{\hphantom{x}}\ \underline{\hphantom{x}}\ \underline{\hphantom{x}}\ \underline{\hphantom{x}}\ \underline{\hphantom{x}}$
   25 9 12 23 9 13 19

3. How did he seem to compose?
   $\underline{\hphantom{x}}\ \underline{\hphantom{x}}\ \underline{\hphantom{x}}\ \underline{\hphantom{x}}\ \underline{\hphantom{x}}\ \underline{\hphantom{x}}\ \underline{\hphantom{x}}\ \underline{\hphantom{x}}\ \underline{\hphantom{x}}\quad \underline{\hphantom{x}}\ \underline{\hphantom{x}}\ \underline{\hphantom{x}}\ \underline{\hphantom{x}}$
   4 24 5 13 4 15 4 1 19   2 9 20 5

4. Where did he win a scholarship?
   $\underline{\hphantom{x}}\ \underline{\hphantom{x}}\ \underline{\hphantom{x}}\ \underline{\hphantom{x}}\ \underline{\hphantom{x}}\ \underline{\hphantom{x}}\ \underline{\hphantom{x}}\ \underline{\hphantom{x}}\ \underline{\hphantom{x}}\ \underline{\hphantom{x}}\ \underline{\hphantom{x}}\ \underline{\hphantom{x}}$
   26 8 12 21 18 26 5 20 16 10 23 1 4

5. Name a composer he revered very much.
   $\underline{\hphantom{x}}\ \underline{\hphantom{x}}\ \underline{\hphantom{x}}\ \underline{\hphantom{x}}\ \underline{\hphantom{x}}\ \underline{\hphantom{x}}\quad \underline{\hphantom{x}}\ \underline{\hphantom{x}}\ \underline{\hphantom{x}}\quad \underline{\hphantom{x}}\ \underline{\hphantom{x}}\ \underline{\hphantom{x}}\ \underline{\hphantom{x}}\ \underline{\hphantom{x}}\ \underline{\hphantom{x}}\ \underline{\hphantom{x}}$
   1 23 7 22 18 14   21 9 12   17 4 4 5 10 8 21 4 1

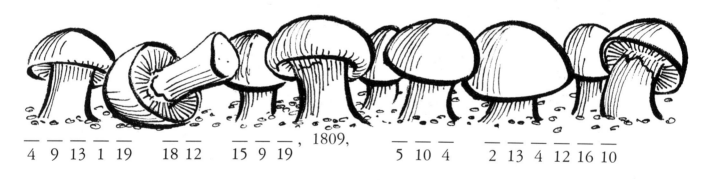

4 9 13 1 19   18 12   15 9 19, 1809,   5 10 4   2 13 4 12 16 10

17 8 15 17 9 13 7 4 7   21 18 4 12 12 9.

4 24 3 4 13 18 4 12 16 18 12 14   5 10 18 20   9 5 5 9 16 26,

22 4 13 4   2 13 9 12 6   20 16 10 23 17 4 13 5,   5 10 4 12

5 22 4 1 21 4   19 4 9 9 13 20   8 1 7,   9 12 7   1 23 7 22 18 14

17 4 4 5 10 8 21 4 12,   22 10 8   22 9 20   5 22 4 12 5 19   20 18 24.

30

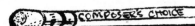

CRYPTIC STORY
Franz Schubert

Each story has a message in substitution code. (One letter of the alphabet has been substituted for the correct letter.) When you have discovered one word, use the known letters to help decode other words. Use the clues!

VIIZTXFIK RXXAIB HZ HVXQZ WNOZD XL WPTQVICZ'W WXKEW BQCNKE ZTI

RHWZ MIIAW XL TNW RNLI. HEHNK HKB HEHNK TI RXXAIB HZ ZTIG,

CISIHZNKE GHKD ZNGIW, ''ZCQRD, NK WPTQVICZ ZTICI BMIRRW H BIFNKI

WSHCA!''

Here are some clues to start you successfully in solving this puzzle. *A* is represented by *H; E* by *I; N* by *K; T* by *Z; G* by *E;* and *S* by *W.*

CHALLENGER CRYPTIC STORY

BYPPYRXAM LJT QTWXUT YB ADSYPTYA KYADSDNLT, LJT WTLLTNAXHJ

MYGTNAWTAL LXMJLTATQ LJT NEPTU YB RJDL YAT WXMJL UDC YN

RNXLT. LJTC NTDPXITQ LJT TOSPYUXGT VEDPXLXTU DAQ SYLTALXDP YB

RYNQU RNXLLTA, USYZTA, DAQ UEAM. XALTPPTHLEDPU DAQ STYSPT XA

LJT DNLU RTNT HPYUTPC RDLHJTQ DAQ LJTXN RYNZU UTGTNTPC

WYAXLYNTQ.

QENXAM LJT CTDN YB 1814, D SYTL BNXTAQ YB UHJEKTNL'U RDU MXGXAM

D SDNLC. UEQQTAPC, LJT SYPXHT SYEAQTQ YA LJT QYYN, XALTNNESLXAM

LJT SDNLC. DPWYUL TGTNCYAT RDU LDZTA LY FDXP. LJT LDPTALTQ SYTL

RDU ZTSL XA FDXP BYN BYENLTTA WYALJU. BNDAI UHJEKTNL RDU

NTPTDUTQ LJT ATOL WYNAXAM; JXU MPDUUTU JDQ KTTA KNYZTA DAQ

JT JDQ D GTNC KPDHZ TCT.

Good luck in this Challenger Cryptic Story! To help you break the code, here are some letters to start you off! *A* is represented by *D; E* by *T; N* by *A; D* by *Q;* and *R* by *N.*

GIUSEPPE VERDI

Giuseppe Verdi was born on October 10, 1813, in Le Roncole, a small village in the Parma area of northern Italy. His father was the village innkeeper and grocer. At an early age Giuseppe showed musical talent. When he was ten years old he was playing the three-manuel organ in the village church.

Success came early in life. When he was twenty-six, his first opera was well-received; his third opera premiered in 1842—and made him famous. Italy was suffering under the oppression of the Austrians, who had invaded their country and ruled in a heartless manner. Verdi's opera *Nabucco* contained a chorus, "Va pensiero, sull'ali dorate," (Fly, thought, on golden wings"). It is sung by Jewish exiles who express their longing for their homes and freedom. The Italians appreciated this longing and took this melody and Verdi to their hearts. This melody became a symbol of resistance against the hated invader. Later, an acrostic was made on his name . . . Vittorio Emanuele Re D'Italia (Victor Emanuel, King of Italy). Victor Emanuel was the man the people wanted to be their king.

Many of the stories of his operas were very poor literary works; he set these melodramatic situations to unforgettable music . . . thus they live. He brought Italian opera to its highest level of development in the 19th century.

The people loved Verdi. A person that was there remarked that it seemed that half of Milan attended his funeral on January 29, 1901. He had requested no music. Suddenly, however, just as a whisper and growing ever louder, a song arose from the people, until at last it was a great swelling of love and grief. The song they were singing was "Va pensiero," the song that had made Verdi a national symbol almost sixty years before.

NOTABLE TRIVIA

In musical markings, *p* stands for *piano,* the Italian word meaning "soft." Verdi used dynamic changes to great effect. However, one would be hard put to follow this marking found in his *Requiem Mass.* . . ppppp. How soft can one get?

GIUSEPPE VERDI
OR
"VIVA VERDI"

```
G I U S E P P E T N Y C
O E D L N A G R O L A E
T O N R A A D I A I A N
T T I O C T T R D Z S S
E E L S U U I O V R R O
L L N S L S P T A E O R
O L R O M E T O I V F S
G O V L R O N C O L E H
I E T A M O L P I D O I
R M E L O D I E S R E P
```

The nine-letter Mystery Word is the name of a Verdi opera.

WORDS TO FIND

Aida, Cairo, censorship, diplomat, Forza, genius, Giuseppe, Italy, Lind, Loss, melodies, opera, organ, *Otello*, political, revolution, *Rigoletto*, Roncole, Rome, tenor, Verdi

GIUSEPPE VERDI

Tie the information together! Social studies and music meet in these facts. Discuss, question and encourage reading and research for deeper understanding of the life of those times.

Happenings in His Life

1813—Giuseppe Verdi is born on October 10, 1813 in Le Roncole, Italy.

1836—Giuseppe marries Margherita Barezzi.

1839—His first opera *Oberto* is presented and well-received.

1842—The opera *Nabucco* with the haunting chorus is produced; Verdi becomes famous.

1851—His opera *Rigoletto* is produced.

1853—*Il Trovatore* and *La Traviata* are produced.

1887—The opera *Otello* is produced.

1901—Verdi dies in Milan, Italy, on January 27.

During That Time in the United States

1813—James Madison is President.

1836—Texan forces at the Alamo are killed by Mexican Army led by General Santa Anna.

1839—The first baseball diamond is laid out in Cooperstown, New York.

1842—Explorer John Fremont leads an expedition to explore a route to Oregon.

1851—Sioux Indians give all their land in Iowa and most of their land in Minnesota to the United States.

1853—Congress authorizes a survey for a transcontinental railroad route to the Pacific.

1887—Pennsylvania Railroad operates an electrically lighted train between Chicago and New York.

1901—McKinley is President; he is shot; Theodore Roosevelt assumes the presidency.

MAKING THE SUBJECT COME ALIVE
(Suggested Activities for Children)
Giuseppe Verdi

1. Interview a singer, choir director or voice teacher and discuss Verdi with them. Get their opinion of his music—if the vocal parts are easy to sing, if the melodies are easy to learn, etc.
2. Find a picture of a willow, an oak and a plane tree. These were some of the trees Verdi chose to plant in his garden.
3. Imagine you are a street cleaner singing one of his songs (or a melody from one of them). Verdi walks down the street and hears you . . . a conversation takes place.
4. Pretend you are a salesman of a new riding lawn mower; try to sell Verdi one. In your persuasive talk bring in all the possible reasons connected with music.

NUMBER WORD GAME
Giuseppe Verdi

Refer to the story section for answers. Place the letters of your answers on the blanks after the clues. Transfer the letters to the same numbered blanks throughout the paragraph below. A story will result.

1. Name the city and country where Verdi was born.

    __ __   __ __ __ __ __ __ __,   __ __ __ __ __
    14 5   3 7 1 22 7 14 5   13 6 15 14 2

2. What profession did his father follow?

    __ __ __ __ __ __ __   __ __ __ __ __ __ __ __ __
    4 13 14 14 15 19 5   13 1 1 21 5 5 17 5 3

3. Give the name of one of his successful operas.

    "__ __ __ __ __ __ __"
     1 15 18 9 22 22 7

4. One of the songs from *Nabucco* expresses the Italians' yearning for something the ruling Austrians would not permit.

    __ __ __ __ __ __ __
    10 3 5 5 12 7 8

5. Why did everyone love Verdi's music? What did it contain?

    __ __ __ __ __ __ __ __ __,   __ __ __ __ __ __ __ __
    20 7 1 12 5 3 10 9 14   11 13 1 19 15 18 14 5

    __ __ __ __ __ __ __ __
    8 5 14 7 12 13 5 11

6. At that time Austrians were . . .

    __ __ __ __ __   __ __ __ __ __ __ __ __ __
    16 15 6 5 12   13 1 4 15 12 5 3 11

__ __ __ __   __ __ __ __ __   __ __ __ __ __ __ __ __ __   __ __
20 16 5 1   4 5 3 12 13   22 7 8 17 14 5 6 5 12   15 1

__ __ __ __ __,   __ __   __ __ __ __ __ __ __   __ __   __ __ __ __.
7 17 5 3 15   16 5   17 14 15 1 6 5 12   15   6 3 5 5

__ __ __ __   __ __ __   __ __   __ __ __ __ __   __ __ __ __   __ __ __
11 7 8 5   15 3 5   15   17 14 15 1 5   6 3 5 5   10 7 3

"__ __ __ __ __ __ __ __ __,"   __ __   __ __ __ __   __ __ __   "__ __
  3 13 19 7 14 5 6 6 7   15 1   7 15 21   10 7 3   13 14

__ __ __ __ __ __ __ __ __,"   __ __   __ __ __ __ __ __ __   __ __ __   "__ __
6 3 7 4 15 6 7 3 5   15   20 13 14 14 7 20   10 7 3   14 15

__ __ __ __ __ __ __ __."
6 3 15 4 13 15 6 15

36

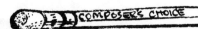

CRYPTIC COMPOSER WORD STORY
Giuseppe Verdi

Each story has a message in substitution code. (One letter of the alphabet has been substituted for the correct letter.) When you have discovered one word, use the known letters to help decode other words. Use the clues!

RAZEB RUIVZQP UQ AZL LBNUQK UYBIG, TBIKZ'L HRU JUOQP LUQL KZBK;

HABQ AZL RZSB KZBK. HAZL HIGPBKJ KBLUEGHBK AZX NUXYEBHBEJ; ZH

LBBXBK QU XOLZN IBXGZQBK ZQ AZL LUOE. G SIZBQK BQNUOIGPBK AZX;

SZQGEEJ, AB RIUHB ''QGWONNU.'' HAZL UYBIG PGTB AUYB HU ZHGEZGQL,

AUYB SUI SIBBKUX SIUX HAB ZQTGKZQP GOLHIZGQ GIXJ. TBIKZ WBNGXB

HABZI ABIU GQK RGL PIBGHEJ EUTBK HAB IBLH US AZL EZSB.

Here are some clues to help you get started on this Verdi Cryptic Story. *A* is represented by *G; E* by *B; H* by *A; M* by *X; O* by *U;* and *T* by *H.*

CHALLENGER CRYPTIC STORY

CWQV IQAMT CFP VTVQNQQV XQFAP SOM, WQ FGGOTQM DSA QVNAFVHQ

NS NWQ BTOFV HSVPQAIFNSAX SD BLPTH. WTP FGGOTHFNTSV CFP

AQEQHNQM. AQFPSVP OFNQA MTPHSIQAQM—HSVPQAIFNSAX

SIQAHASCMQM, WQ CFP F DSAQTKVQA, NSS SOM FVM MTM VSN WSOM

WFVMP HSAAQHNOX TV GTFVS GOFXTVK. XQFAP OFNQA, NWQ

HSVPQAIFNSAX CFVNQM NS RQ VFBQM FDNQA WTB. IQAMT FVPCQAQM

NWQTA AQJLQPN DSA NWTP GQABTPPTSV RX AQBFAZTVK, ''NWQX

CSLOMV'N WFIQ BQ XSLVK. NWQX HFVVSN WFIQ BQ SOM.'' TN CFP OFNQA

VFBQM DSA WTB.

Here are some clues for you in the Challenger Cryptic Story. Good luck in decoding this story! *A* is represented by *F; E* by *Q; L* by *O;* and *N* by *V.*

PETER ILICH TCHAIKOVSKY

Peter Ilich Tchaikovsky was born on May 7, 1840, in Votkinsk. This village is in the Ural Mountains area, 600 miles east of Moscow. As a child he was sensitive to music but was also precocious in other things. At the age of six, he could read French and German. However, he was twenty-one years old before he started the serious study of music.

In composing, he had the gift of melody . . . and what hauntingly beautiful melodies he has given us. *Romeo and Juliet* contains romantically flowing and dramatic music; the music for the ballet *The Nutcracker* is always enchanting.

He is in the period of music classified as Romantic. In this musical period, emotions were dramatically depicted. They were expressed in great extremes of dynamics (loud and soft), sweeping use of the string section, sudden crescendos and diminuendos (gradually getting louder and gradually growing softer), as well as the liberal use of accents. In his *Symphony, No. 6* (sometimes called the *Pathétique) he placed the dynamic markings of pppppp* in one place. The Italian word for soft is *piano (p),* very soft is *pianissimo (pp).* Use your imagination for the interpretation of *pppppp!*

In the late fall of 1893, a cholera epidemic swept through St. Petersburg (now Leningrad). Orders were issued to boil all drinking water. One day, he drank a glassful of water coming right from the water tap; cholera developed. He died a few days later on November 6, 1893. This seemed especially tragic, for almost two weeks earlier his *Symphony No. 6* had a very successful premiere.

NOTABLE TRIVIA
Every night he would like to play the card game of Whist. If nobody would play with him, he would play Solitaire. Cards were a favorite.

PETER TCHAIKOVSKY
OR
"HAUNTINGLY BEAUTIFUL MELODIES"

```
R U S S I A U N P L A Y A B L E M G O
N U T C R A C K E R K B S W A N N D A
O C B F C O M P O S E R Y A S O D O P
T N A I O I T O V E T A M L S L T A A
S O A P N L H O S O V S P T L R T R R
O N E I R S K A I C I S H Z E H H E T
B E N V P I T P L R O S O C E E E L S
A G E D A O C E P L L W N T P A M O E
L I I H E L R C I R A O I O I R E H H
L N C M E K S A I N C Q E Y N T S C C
E T O P E R A H T O U C S U G A R E R
T R E P A K W S M E L O D I E S O L O
```

The eleven-letter Mystery Word is frequently used when describing many of his compositions.

WORDS TO FIND

aged, ballet, Boston, brass, Capriccio, cholera, clerk, composer, concerto, folk, hall, heart, lone, melodies, mining, Moscow, Nutcracker, odd, Onégin, opera, orchestra, *Pathétique*, piano, Piotr, rate, Romeo, Rubinstein, Russia, slave, sleeping, solo, song, sugar, swan, symphonies, themes, toy, Trepak, Tchaikovsky, unplayable, viola, waltz, wants, whirls

PETER ILICH TCHAIKOVSKY

Tie the information together! Social studies and music meet in these facts. Discuss, question and encourage reading and research for deeper understanding of the life of those times.

Happenings in His Life	During That Time in the United States
1840, May 7—Peter Ilich Tchaikovsky is born in Votinsk, Russia.	1840—Texas independence recognized.
1846—Ilich begins speaking French and German.	1846—Abraham Lincoln's second son, Edward Baker Lincoln, is born.
1861—He begins to study music seriously.	1861—The Civil War or War Between the States starts.
1890—He visits New York City to conduct a series of concerts where his works would be played.	1890—Idaho becomes the 43rd state, and Wyoming becomes the 44th state.
1893—On November 6, he dies.	1893—Henry Ford builds the first successful gasoline engine.

MAKING THE SUBJECT COME ALIVE
(Suggested Activities for Children)

Peter Ilich Tchaikovsky

1. Listen to the *Nutcracker Suite*. Pick your favorite piece from this suite and make a report to the class about it. Create any pictures to help your report.
2. Listen to the ''1812'' overture. Read about its sections and try to recognize them after several hearings. Make a report of it.
3. Imagine you are Peter Tchaikovsky and have ideas about a composition you want to start writing, but discover all the music paper has been used. A blizzard is raging outside. How would *you* solve this problem?

NUMBER WORD GAME
Peter Ilich Tchaikovsky

Refer to the story section for answers. Place the letters of your answers on the blanks after the clues. Transfer the letters to the same numbered blanks throughout the paragraph below. A story will result.

1. Who is the composer of the *Nutcracker Suite?*

    ___ ___ ___ ___ ___   ___ ___ ___ ___ ___
    21 1   6   1   4   10 7 10 12 13

    ___ ___ ___ ___ ___ ___ ___ ___ ___ ___ ___
    6 12 13 14 10 18   3 22 20 18   2
    "   "

2. What is his *Symphony No. 6* sometimes called?

    ___ ___ ___ ___ ___ ___ ___ ___ ___ ___
    21 14   6 13   1   6 10 23   8   1

3. What languages did he speak when he was very young?

    ___ ___ ___ ___ ___ ___,   ___ ___ ___ ___ ___ ___
    17   4   1 11 12 13   19   1   4   5 14 11

4. Name the month when he died.

    ___ ___ ___ ___ ___ ___ ___ ___
    11   3 22   1   5 16   1   4

___ ___ 1890,   ___ ___ ___ ___ ___ ___ ___ ___ ___ ___ ___
10 11   6 12 13 14 10 18   3 22 20 18   2

___ ___ ___ ___   ___ ___   ___ ___ ___   ___ ___ ___ ___   ___ ___ ___ ___.
15   1 11   6   6   3   11   1 15   2   3   4 18   12 10   6   2

___ ___   ___ ___ ___   ___ ___ ___ ___ ___ ___ ___   ___ ___   ___ ___ ___
13   1   15 14 20   20   6   8 11 11   1   9   16   2   6 13   1

___ ___ ___ ___ ___ ___ ___ ___ ___ ___ ___.   ___ ___   ___ ___   ___ ___ ___ ___
20 18   2 20 12   4 14 21   1   4 20   13   1   10 20   20 14 10   9

___ ___   ___ ___ ___ ___ ___   ___ ___ ___ ___ ___ ___ ___ ___ ___ ___,   " ___ ___ ___ ___
6   3   13 14 22   1   12   3   5   5   1 11   6   1   9   15 13 14   6

___ ___ ___   ___ ___ ___ ___ ___ ___   ___ ___ ___ ___ ___ ___ ___ ___   ___ ___   ___ ___
14   4   1   21   1   3 21   7   1   6 13 10 11 18 10 11 19   3 17   6   3

___ ___ ___ ___   ___ ___   ___ ___ ___   ___ ___ ___ ___ ___ ___ ___ ___ ___ ___
7 10 22   1   3 11   6 13   1   6 13 10   4   6   1   1 11   6 13

___ ___ ___ ___ ___   ___ ___   ___ ___   ___ ___ ___ ___ ___ ___ ___ ___ ___?"
17   7   3   3   4   3 17   14   16   8 10   7   9 10 11 19

42

CRYPTIC STORY
Peter Ilich Tchaikovsky

Each story has a message in substitution code. (One letter of the alphabet has been substituted for the correct letter.) When you have discovered one word, use the known letters to help decode other words. Use the clues!

JARSAKHVK RGTH PKH AQ GOO WMHU KHH GDZ MHGV GDZ WMVAPYM

WMHXV AND JVHGWXCH YHDXPK RGTH XW WMHXV AND.

WJMGXTACKTU PKHZ QAOT RHOAZXHK XD WMXK NGU. QVAR MXK

NVXWXDYK, MH MGK WAOZ PK WMH KAPVJH AQ KARH AQ WMHKH

XZHGK.

G KADY MH QVHFPHDWOU MHGVZ KPDY LU LOXDZ LHYYGVK AD WMH

KWVHHW LHJGRH G WMHRH XD MXK JADJHVWA XD L QOGW RXDAV GDZ

SXGDA, DA. Q, ASPK 23. G QVXHDZ'K LPWOHV NGK KXDYXDY G SASPOGV

QAOT RHOAZU JGOOHZ ''WMH JVGDH.'' XW GSSHGVK XD WMH QXDGOH

AQ MXK KURSMADU DA. 2 XD J RXDAV, ASPK 17.

Here are some clues to help you get started on this Tchaikovsky Cryptic Story. *A* is represented by *G; C* by *J; E* by *H; H* by *M; O* by *A;* and *T* by *W.* Good luck!

CHALLENGER CRYPTIC STORY

VMOMB OZPGUTHDXTN GSI JBMSZP ZHYVHXMB ZGYUAAM XGUSO-XGMSX

QMBM USDUOMI OH MSCAGSI OH BMZMUDM G IHZOHBGOM JBHY

ZGYRBUICM KSUDMBXUON. XGUSO-XGMSX ZGAAMI PUY OPM

''CMSOAMXO GSI TUSIMXO HJ YMS,'' GAXH BMYGBTUSC OPGO PM QGX G

ZHYVHXMB HJ ''OGAMSO GSI GXOHKSIUSC OMZPSUWKM.''

Here are some clues to help you start this rather difficult cryptic story. *A* is represented by *G; C* by *Z; E* by *M; L* by *A; N* by *S;* and *O* by *H.* Good luck!

JOHN PHILIP SOUSA

John Philip Sousa was born on November 6, 1854, in Washington, D.C. His father was a part-time carpenter for the U.S. Navy and also played the trombone in the U.S. Marine Band. John Philip's early interest in music led to music lessons when he was seven years old. He learned to play the violin, cornet and trombone. At the age of 14, he became an apprentice in the U.S. Marine Band. Jacques Offenbach, a famous French composer, toured the United States with his orchestra and invited John Philip to play the violin with his orchestra. The U.S. Marine Band allowed him to leave to participate in this experience.

In 1878, he married Jennie Bellis. In 1880, he was invited to become the conductor of the U.S. Marine Band. He accepted this honor and for the next twelve years, the U.S. Marine Band reached a new standard of excellence in performance, technique and repertoire. He composed many marches for this band. ''Semper Fidelis'' (always faithful) became the official march of the U.S. Marine Band. Some of his most famous marches are ''El Capitan,'' ''Thunderer,'' ''The Washington Post,'' ''King Cotton,'' and ''The Stars and Stripes Forever.'' He wrote operettas and musicals; however, his marches reached everyone's heart. An English band magazine called him ''The March King''; truly he is. His lively marches are full of catchy melodies, vigor and dash. The use of syncopation (accent on the offbeat), added to the rhythmic excitement; he was one of the first composers to use this type of rhythm in marches.

During the years he was director of the U.S. Marine Band, it performed at most of the official functions at the White House and many of the parties. These were the men who were President during his conductorship: Rutherford B. Hayes, James A. Garfield, Chester Arthur, Grover Cleveland and Benjamin Harrison.

He always wore a new pair of white kid gloves for every performance. He toured the world with his own band and received many, many honors. He died on March 6, 1932, in Reading, Pennsylvania; the day before had been a long one with rehearsals all day.

NOTABLE TRIVIA
He once ordered 1,200 pairs of white kid gloves from a Fifth Avenue store in New York City.

JOHN PHILIP SOUSA OR "THE MARCH KING"

```
C A T C H Y L I M A F S P I R I T E D
C I T O I R T A P A K B E A R D E A E
R T R V S O U S A I R D L M R R L C Z
E H Y C A R T F L A G C E E H A I R I
S G S M U R D L J O H N H T N T D A N
O I R B E S P I C C O L O E N D Y E O
P R E C E P T I O N S O M E R U E H M
M B N R T E I S A T T E R E P O A E R
O O U U U T W E L V E P O S T T R H A
C O N D U C T O R T P H O N O R S Y H
T E Y L E V I L E A D E R E N I R A M
```

The Sousa marches were made more interesting by the use of this seven-letter Mystery Word.

WORDS TO FIND

apprentice, beard, blend, bright, brio, catchy, circus, composer, concerts, conductor, drums, duet, family, flag, harmonized, haunted, hear, hero, honors, John, lad, leader, lively, march, Marine, meet, operettas, parade, patriotic, piccolo, post, receptions, rhythm, skill, Sousa, spirited, three, toot, tour, try, tune, twelve, years

JOHN PHILIP SOUSA

Tie the information together! Social studies and music meet in these facts. Discuss, question and encourage reading and research for deeper understanding of the life of those times.

Happenings in His Life

1854—John Philip Sousa is born on November 6, 1854.

1876—He becomes a "principal" musician in the U.S. Marine Band in Washington, D.C.

1878—John Philip marries Jennie Bellis.

1880—He becomes the conductor of the U.S. Marine Band in Washington, D.C.

1885—His most successful operetta *El Capitan* is produced.

1892—He leaves the U.S. Marine Band to create his own band and tour with it.

1896—He writes "The Stars and Stripes Forever."

1932—On March 6, 1932, he dies.

During That Time in the United States

1854—Franklin Pierce is President of the United States.

1876—The Battle of Little Bighorn takes place. General George Custer and many cavalrymen are killed by Sioux and Cheyenne Indians.

1878—The first bicycles are manufactured; they are called "wheels."

1880—James A. Garfield is elected President.

1885—The Statue of Liberty is lighted.

1892—Katherine Lee Bates writes a poem, "America, the Beautiful."

1896—Utah becomes the 45th state.

1932—Franklin D. Roosevelt is elected President.

MAKING THE SUBJECT COME ALIVE
(Suggested Activities for Children)
John Philip Sousa

1. Listen to "The Stars and Stripes Forever." Discover the various sections; try to identify the instruments that have solo parts. Show pictures of the instruments as they are heard. This report could be made by a group of children . . . each using his own talents.
2. Imagine you are John Philip Sousa trying to find a clean pair of white kid gloves for your concert that should start soon. You could create all sorts of problems—he finds two gloves, but both for the same hand . . . two gloves that match, except one has a hole in one of the fingers . . . two matching gloves, except one is long and the other short . . . etc.
3. After solving the puzzle about John Philip Sousa getting ideas for "The Stars and Stripes Forever," dramatize it yourself, making this bit of history the way you think it might have happened.
4. Listen to the march "The Thunderer." Be a tune detective and discover how many beats in a measure; try to direct it as the record is played.

NUMBER WORD GAME
John Philip Sousa

Refer to the story section for answers. Place the letters of your answers on the blanks after the clues. Transfer the letters to the same numbered blanks throughout the paragraph below. A story will result.

1. Name the city where John Philip Sousa was born.

   $\overline{3}\ \overline{8}\ \overline{12}\ \overline{1}\ \overline{19}\ \overline{2}\ \overline{7}\ \overline{21}\ \overline{17}\ \overline{2},\ \ \overline{18}.\ \ \overline{14}.$

2. How old was he when he became a Marine apprentice?

   $\overline{20}\ \overline{17}\ \overline{15}\ \overline{9}\ \overline{21}\ \overline{6}\ \overline{6}\ \overline{2}$

3. Give his official title.

   $\overline{14}\ \overline{17}\ \overline{2}\ \overline{18}\ \overline{15}\ \overline{14}\ \overline{21}\ \overline{17}\ \overline{9}\ \ \overline{17}\ \overline{20}\ \ \overline{21}\ \overline{1}\ \overline{6}\ \ \overline{4}\ \overline{8}\ \overline{9}\ \overline{19}\ \overline{2}\ \overline{6}$

   $\overline{10}\ \overline{8}\ \overline{2}\ \overline{18}$

4. What he was called by an admiring public

   $\overline{21}\ \overline{1}\ \overline{6}\ \ \overline{4}\ \overline{8}\ \overline{9}\ \overline{14}\ \overline{1}\ \ \overline{5}\ \overline{19}\ \overline{2}\ \overline{7}$

5. Give this composer's full name.

   $\overline{22}\ \overline{17}\ \overline{1}\ \overline{2}\ \ \overline{13}\ \overline{1}\ \overline{19}\ \overline{16}\ \overline{19}\ \overline{13}\ \ \overline{12}\ \overline{17}\ \overline{15}\ \overline{12}\ \overline{8}$

6. He wore a new pair of these at every performance.

   $\overline{3}\ \overline{1}\ \overline{19}\ \overline{21}\ \overline{6}\ \ \overline{5}\ \overline{19}\ \overline{18}\ \ \overline{7}\ \overline{16}\ \overline{17}\ \overline{23}\ \overline{6}\ \overline{12}$

7. Give the name of the state in which he died.

   $\overline{13}\ \overline{6}\ \overline{2}\ \overline{2}\ \overline{12}\ \overline{11}\ \overline{16}\ \overline{23}\ \overline{8}\ \overline{2}\ \overline{19}\ \overline{8}$

ACME BANDMASTER BATON CORP.

$\overline{9}\ \overline{6}\ \overline{21}\ \overline{15}\ \overline{9}\ \overline{2}\ \overline{19}\ \overline{2}\ \overline{7}\ \ \overline{10}\ \overline{11}\ \ \overline{12}\ \overline{1}\ \overline{19}\ \overline{13}\ \ \overline{20}\ \overline{9}\ \overline{17}\ \overline{4}$

$\overline{6}\ \overline{15}\ \overline{9}\ \overline{17}\ \overline{13}\ \overline{6}\ \ \overline{19}\ \overline{2}\ $ 1896, $\ \overline{22}\ \overline{17}\ \overline{1}\ \overline{2}\ \ \overline{13}\ \overline{1}\ \overline{19}\ \overline{16}\ \overline{19}\ \overline{13}$

$\overline{12}\ \overline{17}\ \overline{15}\ \overline{12}\ \overline{8}\ \ \overline{12}\ \overline{21}\ \overline{9}\ \overline{17}\ \overline{16}\ \overline{16}\ \overline{6}\ \overline{18}\ \ \overline{8}\ \overline{10}\ \overline{17}\ \overline{15}\ \overline{21}\ \ \overline{21}\ \overline{1}\ \overline{6}$

$\overline{18}\ \overline{6}\ \overline{14}\ \overline{5}.\ \ \overline{8}\ \ \overline{4}\ \overline{6}\ \overline{16}\ \overline{17}\ \overline{18}\ \overline{11}\ \ \overline{20}\ \overline{16}\ \overline{17}\ \overline{8}\ \overline{21}\ \overline{6}\ \overline{18}\ \ \overline{19}\ \overline{2}\ \overline{21}\ \overline{17}\ \ \overline{1}\ \overline{19}\ \overline{12}$

$\overline{4}\ \overline{19}\ \overline{2}\ \overline{18}\ \ \overline{8}\ \overline{12}\ \ \overline{1}\ \overline{6}\ \ \overline{12}\ \overline{8}\ \overline{3}\ \ \text{``}\ \overline{17}\ \overline{16}\ \overline{18}\ \ \overline{7}\ \overline{16}\ \overline{17}\ \overline{9}\ \overline{11}\ \text{''}$

$\overline{20}\ \overline{16}\ \overline{11}\ \overline{19}\ \overline{2}\ \overline{7}\ \ \overline{8}\ \overline{21}\ \ \overline{21}\ \overline{1}\ \overline{6}\ \ \overline{12}\ \overline{21}\ \overline{6}\ \overline{9}\ \overline{2}\ \ \overline{17}\ \overline{20}\ \ \overline{21}\ \overline{1}\ \overline{6}$

$\overline{12}\ \overline{1}\ \overline{19}\ \overline{13}\ \ \overline{19}\ \overline{21}\ \ \overline{18}\ \overline{6}\ \overline{23}\ \overline{6}\ \overline{16}\ \overline{17}\ \overline{13}\ \overline{6}\ \overline{18}\ \ \overline{19}\ \overline{2}\ \overline{21}\ \overline{17}$

$\text{``}\ \overline{21}\ \overline{1}\ \overline{6}\ \ \overline{12}\ \overline{21}\ \overline{8}\ \overline{9}\ \overline{12}\ \ \overline{8}\ \overline{2}\ \overline{18}\ \ \overline{12}\ \overline{21}\ \overline{9}\ \overline{19}\ \overline{13}\ \overline{6}\ \overline{12}\ \ \overline{20}\ \overline{17}\ \overline{9}\ \overline{6}\ \overline{23}\ \overline{6}\ \overline{9}\ \text{''}$

CRYPTIC STORY

John Philip Sousa

Each story has a message in substitution code. (One letter of the alphabet has been substituted for the correct letter.) When you have discovered one word, use the known letters to help decode other words. Use the clues!

TYWJ SWDADS ZYPZE'Z KELWQF'Z JEXQ REZ EJLYJDY ZY (WDZ KEXDAI REZ

ZSEJDZW). E ZLYFI DZ LYAH LWEL TYWJ SWDADS ZYPZE EHHQH P.Z.E. LY DL;

LWPZ LWQ JEXQ ZYPZE REZ VFQELQH.

Note: To help you, here are some letters and the ones they represent. Good luck in breaking the code! *E* is represented by *Q; R* by *F; N* by *J; S* by *Z; A* by *E.*

CHALLENGER CRYPTIC STORY

PSQI MSQHSPIB'P QJPRM RP RVPWTVWYA BIMSDVRKIL—T GTYWK EA

USNTVV PWBTJPP 11, T MSQHSPRWRSV EA GSYZDTVD TQTLIJP QSKTBW SB T

QTBMN EA USNV HNRYRH PSJPT. WNBSJDN WNIRB FIBA SGV WTYIVWP, WNIA

MBITWIL T PWAYI TVL RVLRFRLJTYRWA WNTW GTP LRPWRVMWRFIYA

WNIRB SGV. PSJPT'P QTBMNIP NTFI T FIBFI, KIPW TVL PHRBRW WNTW YRZW

SJB IQSWRSVP. NI BTRPIL WNI QTBMN TVL ETVL QJPRM WS NITBW-PWRBBRVD

NIRDNWP.

In this rather difficult cryptic story, here are some clues to get you started. *A* is represented by *T; E* by *I; O* by *S; M* by *Q, N* by *V;* and *S* by *P.*

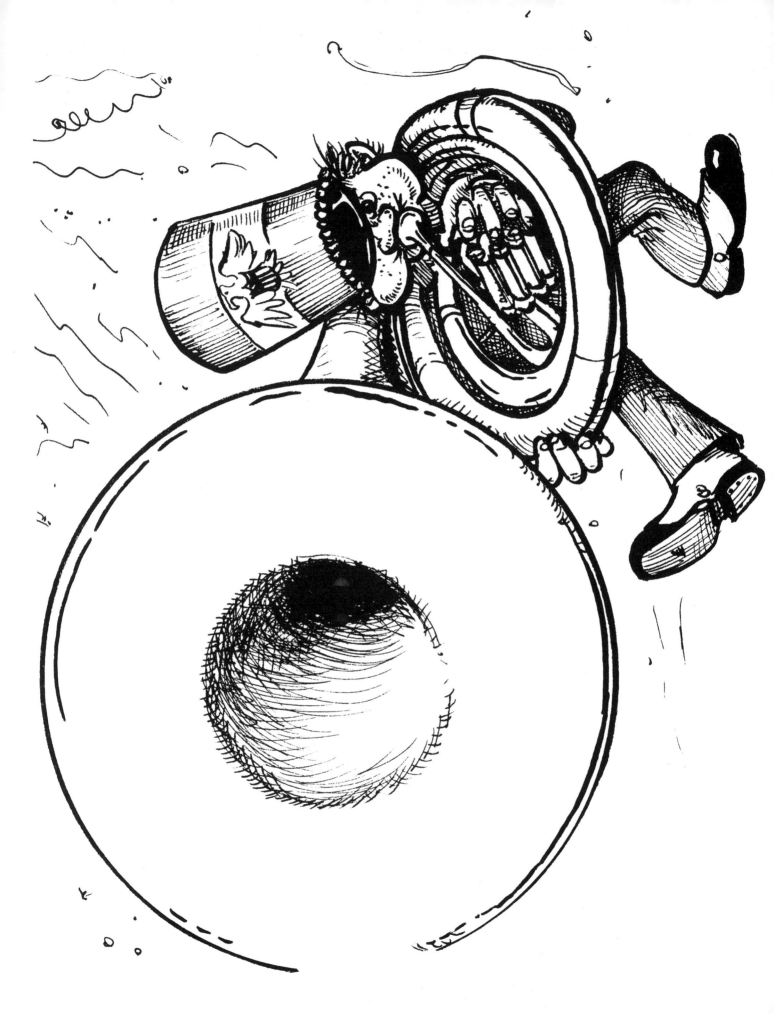

SERGEI PROKOFIEV

Sergei Prokofiev was born on April 23, 1891, in the village of Sontsovka, in the Ukraine, now a part of Russia. His father managed a large estate in this area of the steppes. An accomplished musician, his mother recognized his musical talent early and was his first teacher. When he was five years old, he was composing piano music; this talent continued and developed. St. Petersburg Conservatory of Music accepted him as a student when he was thirteen years old. Ten years later he graduated and received the Rubinstein Prize for his piano playing. He was a virtuoso! How rebellious he was. He said exactly what he thought and did not respect other musicians or composers. An early stage he went through was the one of percussive piano playing. He said the piano was a percussion instrument and should be played like one. Compositions written during this time were mocking, violent . . . very anti-romantic. The driving rhythm and dissonance were intended to shock; they did. Someone remarked that he was either hated or admired, never overlooked.

The Russian Revolution of 1917 caused him to flee to the United States, where the expected success did not develop. After three years he moved to Paris, France, continuing to compose and conduct. In 1933, he returned to live in Russia and draw upon his ''roots'' for inspiration. This twentieth century composer wrote in a variety of forms—chamber music, cantatas, music for the movies and theater, sonatas, concertos for various instruments, operas and symphonies.

When he incurred the displeasure of the Central Committee of the Communist Party in 1948, a very unpleasant three days resulted. A spokesman from the Politburo lectured to Prokofiev, Shostakovich and Katchaturian all this time! Prokofiev sat with his back to the speaker. Finally, when it ended, they apologized. No outstanding compositions followed.

Some of his most popular works are *Peter and the Wolf, Classical Symphony,* and the ballet music for *Romeo and Juliet.* He died on March 5, 1953, a respected modern composer that made a contribution to twentieth century music.

NOTABLE TRIVIA

Musician-like, he remembered telephone numbers by their intonation.

SERGEI PROKOFIEV
OR
"TALENT . . . TROUBLE . . . AND A FAIRY TALE"

```
P  R  O  K  O  F  I  E  V  S  E  P  K  W  D
I  O  M  O  D  E  R  N  Y  O  Z  B  I  O  I
O  S  P  A  R  I  S  M  P  F  I  E  J  C  S
N  L  E  U  U  E  P  E  L  T  G  S  I  S  S
E  Y  T  V  L  H  R  O  T  R  O  O  R  O  O
E  S  E  U  O  A  W  E  E  C  L  V  U  M  N
R  I  R  N  K  L  R  S  T  B  O  I  S  A  A
B  O  Y  K  S  V  E  N  A  I  P  E  S  R  N
A  N  T  I  D  E  M  O  C  R  A  T  I  C  T
S  O  N  T  S  O  V  K  A  D  F  L  A  H  Y
```

This six-letter Mystery Word describing Prokofiev means resourceful, courageous and daring.

WORDS TO FIND

antidemocratic, apologize, bird, bitter, boy, cat, dissonant, half, Kiji, loves, march, modern, Moscow, Nevsky, noisy, opera, Paris, Peter, pioneer, popular, Prokofiev, rules, Russia, Sergei, Sontsovka, Soviet, symphony, wolf

SERGEI PROKOFIEV

Tie the information together. Social studies and music meet in these facts. Discuss, question and encourage reading and research for deeper understanding of the life of those times.

Happenings in His Life

1904—Sergei enters the St. Petersburg Conservatory of Music.

1914—He graduates from the St. Petersburg Conservatory of Music.

1917—The Russian Revolution causes him to flee to the United States.

1933—He returns to Russia to live.

1936—*Peter and the Wolf* is composed.

1948, February 10—Prokofiev and other Russian composers are lectured to for three days by a spokesman from the Politburo.

1953—Sergei Prokofiev dies on March 5.

During That Time in the United States

1904—Theodore Roosevelt is elected President.

1914—*Tarzan of the Apes* by Edgar R. Burroughs is published.

1917—United States declares war on Germany.

1933—The Empire State Building, with its 102 stories, is two years old.

1936—Franklin D. Roosevelt is reelected President.

1948—CBS produces the first color telecast.

1953—The New York Yankees defeat the Brooklyn Dodgers in the World Series for the fifth time in a row!

MAKING THE SUBJECT COME ALIVE
Sergei Prokofiev

1. Listen carefully to *Peter and the Wolf*. Notice how the music reflects the personality of the person or animal (jaunty, confident for Peter, etc.). Discuss in class and decide what words describe each person or animal.
2. Read about the life of Prokofiev. Pick one phase, or any part of it you like, and make a report. Share it with the class.
3. Make the scene you like from *Peter and the Wolf* in a shadow box, shoe box or any type of firm background. Use pipe cleaners, clothespins or small dolls and animal toys for the characters or make your own.

NUMBER WORD GAME
Sergei Prokofiev

Refer to the story section for answers. Place the letters of your answers on the blanks after the clues. Transfer the letters to the same numbered blanks throughout the paragraph below. A story will result.

1. Name the village and country where Sergei was born.

   __ __ __ __ __ __ __ __ __, __ __ __ __ __ __
   2 9 3 7 2 9 19 8 20   4 12 2 2 21 20

2. Name the music school he entered at the age of 13.

   __ __. __ __ __ __ __ __ __ __ __ __
   2 7   1 5 7 5 4 2 22 12 4 13

   __ __ __ __ __ __ __ __ __ __ __ __ __ __ __ __ __ __ __
   17 9 3 2 5 4 19 20 7 9 4 16 9 10 15 12 2 21 17

3. Children like this composition of his. "__ __ __ __ __ __ __ __ __ __ __ __ __ __ __"
   1 5 7 5 4   20 3 18   7 11 5   6 9 14 10

4. This group was displeased with his work.

   __ __ __ __ __ __ __ __ __ __ __ __ __ __ __ __
   17 5 3 7 4 20 14   17 9 15 15 21 7 7 5 5

   __ __ __ __ __ __ __ __ __ __ __ __ __ __ __ __ __ __ __
   9 10   7 11 5   17 9 15 15 12 3 21 2 7   1 20 4 7 16

"__ __ __ __ __ __ __ __ __ __ __ __ __ __ __" __ __ __
 1 5 7 5 4   20 3 18   7 11 5   6 9 14 10   6 20 2

__ __ __ __ __ __ __ __ __ __ __ __ __ __ __ __. __ __
6 4 21 7 7 5 3   21 3   9 3 5   6 5 5 8   11 5

__ __ __ __ __ __ __ __ __ __ __ __ __ __ __ __ __ __ __ __ __ __ __
17 9 3 18 12 17 7 5 18   7 11 21 2   9 4 17 11 5 2 7 4 20 14

__ __ __ __ __ __ __ __ __ __ __ __ __ __ __ __ __ __ __ __ __ __ __ __ __
6 9 4 8   20 7   21 7 2   10 21 4 2 7   1 5 4 10 9 4 15 20 3 17 5

__ __ __ __ __ __ __ __ __ __ __ __ __ __ __ __ __ __ __ __ __ __ __
20 7   20 3   20 10 7 5 4 3 9 9 3   17 9 3 17 5 4 7   10 9 4

__ __ __ __ __ __ __ __ __ __ __ __ __ 2, 1936, __ __ __ __ __
17 11 21 14 18 4 5 3   9 3   15 20 16   20 7   7 11 5

__ __ __ __ __ __ __ __ __, __ __ __ __ __ __ __ __ __ __ __ __ __ __ __ __.
17 11 21 14 18 4 5 3 2   7 11 5 20 7 5 4   21 3   15 9 2 17 9 6

54

CRYPTIC STORY
Sergei Prokofiev

Each story has a message in substitution code. (One letter of the alphabet has been substituted for the correct letter.) When you have discovered one word, use the known letters to help decode other words. Use the clues!

OMRWRKRW MR ORPX, TWAZAHQRK VDWWQRL PAXRNAAZE XA OWQXR

QLRDE, FRUALQRE DPL XMRFRE AH FYEQV. EAFRXQFRE XMRS VDFR OMRP MR

ODE RDXQPJ, ODUZQPJ, QP NRL AW DPSOMRWR! OMRP MR EXDWXRL D PRO

VAFTAEQXQAP, XMRER ORWR QPKDUYDNUR. JRPRWDUUS, MR VAFTAERL

NRXORRP XRP QP XMR FAWPQPJ DPL PAAP.

Note: Good luck in breaking the code! To give you a start, here are some of the letters and those representing them. *A* is represented by *D; E* by *R; N* by *P; S* by *E* and *R* by *W; I* by *Q; H* by *M.*

CHALLENGER CRYPTIC STORY

YAMZ UNWPWDRMS YHI YWNPRZT, AM VRPMJ BW AHSM IWCM XHZJO WZ

ARI JMIP. AM HVYHOI XHNNRMJ IWCM RZ ARI UWXPMBI. AM YHI HVYHOI

BNORZT HZJ XNMHBRZT ZMY BARZTI. IWCM YMNM ILXXMIIDLV, IWCM

DHRVLNMI. WZM LZLILHV XNMHBRWZ YHI H ZMY YHO WD YNRBRZT—

YRBAWLB SWYMVI!

This Challenger Cryptic Story may be a bit difficult . . . not many clues this time. Here are the clues. *A* is represented by *H; E* by *M; N* by *Z;* and *O* by *W.* Good luck!

PERSONALITIES
IN THE ARTS

Mikhail Baryshnikov
Luciano Pavarotti
Itzhak Perlman
Mstislav Rostropovich
Andrés Segovia
Beverly Sills
Joan Sutherland

MIKHAIL BARYSHNIKOV

Mikhail Baryshnikov was born on January 27, 1948, in Riga, Latvia, now a part of the Soviet Union. He was raised by his grandmother and his father, a Soviet officer. Until he was introduced to ballet by chance, he was an eager participant in soccer games and other sports. The excellent Riga Dance School training merely polished his superb inborn coordination, balance precision and musicality. He joined the Kirov Ballet Company, and it was in this ballet company that he made his debut in 1967. He stood out among the dancers because of his astonishing energy and speed of execution. He is a perfectionist and possesses a youthful charm and confidence; his phenomenal technique has never been surpassed. In 1969, he received a gold medal for performance at the International Ballet Competition in Moscow. In 1973, he received the title of Honored Artist of the U.S.S.R. His intellectual curiosity helped him become conscious of the provinciality of the Soviet culture. After 1917, many great Russian artistic traditions were forbidden. In June 1974, the Kirov Ballet was touring Canada. In Toronto, he asked for and received political asylum. Performances with the Canadian ballet companies followed. He arrived in New York City and became ballet's new idol after three performances. Upon joining the American Ballet Company, he learned twenty-six new roles in two years! In 1980 he was named Artistic Director of the American Ballet Theatre.

NOTABLE TRIVIA
Fishing is his favorite pastime!

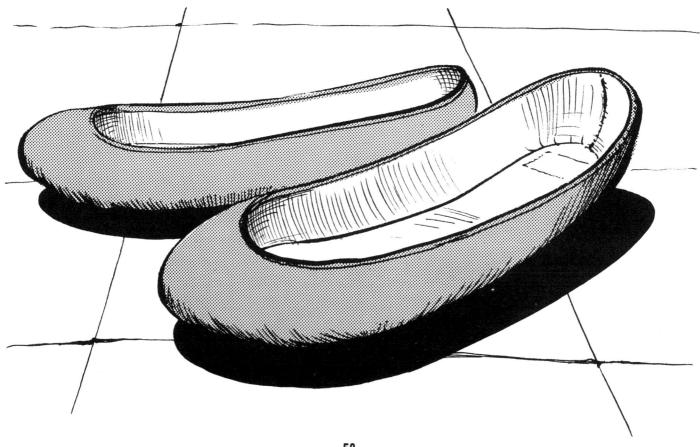

MIKHAIL BARYSHNIKOV
OR
"ELEGANCE IN MOTION"

WORDS TO FIND

afar, aid, aim, ballet, Baryshnikov, born, dance, dazzling, dedication, defection, directing, eats, fair, films, gifted, graceful, guest, intense, intricate, Kirov, leaps, Petipa, rehearsed, roles, Russian, soaring, spins, superstar, stage, talent, taste, untiring

The ten-letter Mystery Word indicates the degree of technical skill he has developed.

```
D E D I C A T I O N S N I P S
E I F A I R K I R O V D E O U
F G R A C E F U L O A T A D P
E I S E L O R V K Z I R F E E
C N P I C R S I Z P I G I S R
T T A D T T N L A N M N L R S
I E E I A H I E G I U I M A T
O N L G S N T N A I D R S E A
N S E Y G S C O G S F I T H R
R E R I A G U E S T T T A E A
O A E T A C I R T N I N E R F
B A L L E T N E L A T U Y D A
```

MIKHAIL BARYSHNIKOV

Tie the information together. Social studies and music meet in these facts. Discuss, question and encourage reading and research for deeper understanding of the life of those times.

Happenings in His Life

1948—Mikhail is born on January 27, in Riga, Latvia (now a part of Russia).

1960—He enters ballet class at Riga Dance School at age twelve.

1967—He makes his debut in the Kirov Ballet company in Leningrad.

1969—Mikhail receives a gold medal in the International Ballet Competition in Moscow.

1973—Mikhail receives the Honored Artist Award of the U.S.S.R.

1974—While touring with the Kirov Ballet company, he asks for and receives political asylum in Toronto, Canada.

1976—He joins the American Ballet Company in New York City.

1980—He becomes Artistic Director of the American Ballet Theatre.

During That Time in the United States

1948—Idlewild Airport in New York City is dedicated, later being renamed John F. Kennedy International Airport.

1960—Senator John F. Kennedy is elected 35th President.

1967—Computers are used to create electronic music.

1969—The World Series is won by the New York Mets in five games.

1973—Rabies vaccine is developed.

1974—Girls are accepted as baseball players in Little League Baseball.

1976—United States celebrates its 200th birthday.

1980—A new 15-cent stamp is used for the first time.

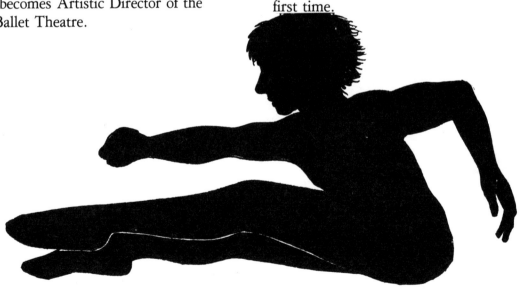

MAKING THE SUBJECT COME ALIVE
(Suggested Activities for Children)
Mikhail Baryshnikov

1. Read a book about ballet dancing that shows the various positions of the feet, hands and body. Try them.
2. Discover what *political asylum* means. What does one have to do to receive it?
3. Make a map of the Union of Soviet Socialist Republics. Locate Riga, (formerly in Latvia), Leningrad and Moscow.

NUMBER WORD GAME
Mikhail Baryshnikov

Refer to the story section for answers. Place the letters of your answers on the blanks after the clues. Transfer the letters to the same numbered blanks throughout the paragraph below. A story will result.

1. Give the first and last names of this suberb ballet dancer.

__ __ __ __ __ __ __ __ __ __ __ __ __ __ __ __ __
9 20 4 17 16 20 7   10 16 13 14 11 17 1 20 4 12 2

2. Name the city and country where he was born.

__ __ __ __, __ __ __ __ __ __
13 20 6 16   7 16 5 2 20 16

3. For his performance at this competition he received a gold medal.

__ __ __ __ __ __ __ __ __ __ __ __ __
20 1 5 3 13 1 16 5 20 12 1 16 7

__ __ __ __ __   __ __ __ __ __ __ __ __ __ __
10 16 7 7 3 5   18 12 9 24 3 5 20 5 20 12 1

4. Give the number of roles he learned in two years.

__ __ __ __ __ __ - __ __ __
5 8 3 1 5 14   11 20 23

5. What position was he was given in 1980?

__ __ __ __ __ __ __ __   __ __ __ __ __ __ __ __
16 13 5 20 11 5 20 18   15 20 13 3 18 5 12 13

__ __   __ __ __   __ __ __ __ __ __ __ __   __ __ __ __ __ __ __
12 22   5 17 3   16 9 3 13 20 18 16 1   10 16 7 7 3 5   5 17 3 16 5 13 3

6. He is famous for performing these in his dancing.

__ __ __ __ __ __ __   __ __ __ __ __   __ __ __
11 12 16 13 20 1 6   7 3 16 24 11   16 1 15

__ __ __ __ __
19 21 9 24 11

__ __ __ __   __ __   __ __ __ __ __ __ __   __ __ __ __
8 17 3 1   17 3   13 3 5 20 13 3 11   22 13 12 9

__ __ __ __ __ __ __, " __ __ __ __ __ " __ __ __ __ __   __ __   __ __ __ __ __
15 16 1 18 20 1 6   9 20 11 17 16   24 7 16 1 11   5 12   3 1 19 12 14

__ __ __   __ __ __ __   __ __   __ __ __ __ __ __ __ __ __ __   __ __
17 20 11   17 12 9 3   20 1   18 12 1 1 3 18 5 20 18 21 5   17 3

__ __ __   __ __ __   __ __ __ __,   __   __ __ __ __ __ __ __
17 16 11   5 8 12   15 12 6 11   16   6 12 7 15 3 1

__ __ __ __ __ __ __ __ __   __ __ __ __ __   __ __ __ __ __   __ __ __   __
13 3 5 13 20 3 2 3 13   1 16 9 3 15   4 16 5 20 16   16 1 15   16

__ __ __ __ __   __ __ __ __ __ __ __   __ __ __ __ __   __ __ __ __ __ __ .
10 7 16 18 4   24 12 12 15 7 3   1 16 9 3 15   6 12 21 7 21 3

61

CRYPTIC STORY
Mikhail Baryshnikov

Each story has a message in substitution code. (One letter of the alphabet has been substituted for the correct letter.) When you have discovered one word, use the known letters to help decode other words. Use the clues!

CG USJ GMPJ LEJS EJ LCX ZMIMSR MS ZJSMSRVCT, EJ ECT C SMHJ

CWCVGPJSG US GEJ PUMQC HCSCZ. VYXXMCS WUJG CZJBCSTJV WYXEQMS

ECT ZMIJT VMREG CHVUXX GEJ LCO TYVMSR GEJ ZCXG TCOX UN EMX

ZMNJ.

Good luck! *A* is represented by *C; E* by *J; N* by *S,* and *R* by *V.*

CHALLENGER CRYPTIC STORY

SQWLEQO YFSCGQSCY YSFWCY E TQTC. QU 1979, LC KCHCQACJ EU LFUFKEKZ

JFHGFKEGC FM MQUC EKGY MKFS ZEOC. DESCY HERUCZ QY LQY LCKF.

Good luck in decoding! *A* is represented by *E; E* by *C; R* by *K;* and *O* by *F.*

LUCIANO PAVAROTTI

Luciano Pavarotti was born on October 12, 1935, in Modena, Italy. This city in north-central Italy is just north of Bologna. His father, a baker, has a very beautiful voice and sings in public to this very day.

Luciano is a tenor (the highest voice part for a man). He has sung in opera houses all over the world as well as giving solo recitals. In 1980, he starred in the movie *Yes, Giorgio!* He has often appeared on TV.

Carrying a handkerchief during a recital or concert has become a hallmark of his. It started as a means of keeping himself in one spot and not waving his hands and arms when immersed in the music. Once he witnessed a colleague making useless movements and actions. It was then he decided a white flag floating around would catch his eye and stop needless action; thus the hand-kerchief.

NOTABLE TRIVIA

Unless he has found a bent nail on the opera stage floor, he does not like to sing. He puts it in his pocket and is then ready to go on stage. This good luck talisman is the result of combining two old Italian superstitions—metal for good luck and horns to ward off evil. The result—wonderful performances and often a hole torn in his pocket.

LUCIANO PAVAROTTI OR "TENOR SUPREME"

```
C O N C E N T R A T I O N K I
A O A N B E A R I R T M E O N
R S M R A H C T O A E G W O T
E O A P K L T N L M A M I G O
E G L I E O E L O T Y R N N N
R D R E R T V R S L T O W I A
A D A A S A I O A A S F O O T
T R V D L Z T T I E R R R G I
S A D U E T I O I C D E K T O
P H R A S I N G N O E P P U N
A N E D O M T A L E N T G O E
```

The nine-letter Mystery Word is something possessed in many fields by this singer.

WORDS TO FIND

arias, baker, bear, career, charm, competition, concentration, dad, duet, hard, intonation, Italy, large, man, memorize, Modena, operas, outgoing, Pavarotti, perform, phrasing, roles, solo, song, stage, star, talent, tall, tenor, tone, trio, voice, work

LUCIANO PAVAROTTI

Tie the information together. Social studies and music meet in these facts. Discuss, question and encourage reading and research for deeper understanding of the life of those times.

Happenings in His Life

1935—Luciano Pavarotti is born in Modena, Italy, on October 12.

1940—Luciano discovers he has a voice!

1943—The Pavarotti family leaves Modena to escape WWII bombings of Italy.

1954—He discovers he has perfect pitch when he starts vocal study seriously.

1961—On April 29, he makes his operatic debut. He marries Adua Veroni in September.

1965—Luciano sings at La Scala Opera House in Milan, Italy. He also sings in America for the first time.

1980—He appears in several television specials.

1981—*Yes, Giorgio,* Luciano's first movie, appears.

During That Time in the United States

1935—In Crosley Field, in Cincinnati, the first major league night baseball game is played by the Cincinnati Reds and the Philadelphia Phillies.

1940—Franklin D. Roosevelt is President.

1943—General Dwight D. Eisenhower is named supreme commander of Allied Expeditionary Force. Its mission is the invasion of western Europe.

1954—Plastic contact lenses are developed.

1961—A vast space program is started; its aim . . . "landing an American on the moon in this decade." John Kennedy is President.

1965—Edward White is the first American to walk in space.

1980—Mount St. Helens erupts! It is a volcano in Washington state.

1981—Ronald Reagan is President.

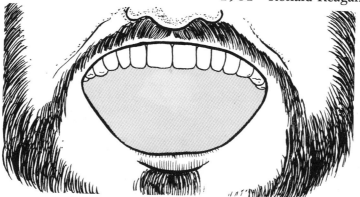

MAKING THE SUBJECT COME ALIVE
(Suggested Activities for Children)
Luciano Pavarotti

1. Invite a tenor to come and sing for your class.
2. Make an operatic shadow box scene, showing the singers on the stage, prompters, chorus, orchestra, orchestra conductor and any other people you think necessary.
3. Pretend you are Luciano looking for a bent nail on the opera stage before a performance. Avoid stagehands, scenery, actors, etc.
4. Make a map of Italy. Locate Modena, Bologna, Rome and Pesaro.
5. Imagine you are ready to go on stage for a performance; you can't find one of your shoes. Solve this problem.

NUMBER WORD GAME
Luciano Pavarotti

Refer to the story section for answers. Place the letters of your answers on the blanks after the clues. Transfer the letters to the same numbered blanks throughout the paragraph below. A story will result.

1. Give this singer's full name.
    $\overline{6}\ \overline{21}\ \overline{15}\ \overline{20}\ \overline{7}\ \overline{14}\ \overline{3}$ $\overline{8}\ \overline{7}\ \overline{4}\ \overline{7}\ \overline{1}\ \overline{3}\ \overline{10}\ \overline{10}\ \overline{20}$

2. Name the town and country where he was born.
    $\overline{13}\ \overline{3}\ \overline{5}\ \overline{18}\ \overline{14}\ \overline{7}$, $\overline{20}\ \overline{10}\ \overline{7}\ \overline{6}\ \overline{19}$

3. What does he always carry when giving a recital?
    $\overline{9}\ \overline{2}\ \overline{20}\ \overline{10}\ \overline{18}$ $\overline{2}\ \overline{7}\ \overline{14}\ \overline{5}\ \overline{11}\ \overline{18}\ \overline{1}\ \overline{15}\ \overline{2}\ \overline{20}\ \overline{18}\ \overline{17}$

4. Name locations where he has sung.
    $\overline{7}\ \overline{6}\ \overline{6}$ $\overline{3}\ \overline{4}\ \overline{18}\ \overline{1}$ $\overline{10}\ \overline{2}\ \overline{18}$ $\overline{9}\ \overline{3}\ \overline{1}\ \overline{6}\ \overline{5}$

5. Give the movie in which he starred. "$\overline{19}\ \overline{18}\ \overline{16}$, $\overline{22}\ \overline{20}\ \overline{3}\ \overline{1}\ \overline{22}\ \overline{20}\ \overline{3}$!"

6. What good luck talisman does he search for before a performance?
    $\overline{23}\ \overline{18}\ \overline{14}\ \overline{10}$ $\overline{14}\ \overline{7}\ \overline{20}\ \overline{6}$

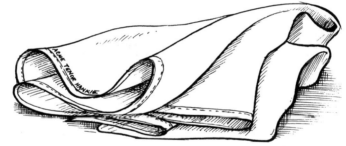

$\overline{6}\ \overline{21}\ \overline{15}\ \overline{20}\ \overline{7}\ \overline{14}\ \overline{3}$ $\overline{8}\ \overline{7}\ \overline{4}\ \overline{7}\ \overline{1}\ \overline{3}\ \overline{10}\ \overline{10}\ \overline{20}$ $\overline{6}\ \overline{20}\ \overline{11}\ \overline{18}\ \overline{16}$

$\overline{10}\ \overline{3}$ $\overline{5}\ \overline{1}\ \overline{20}\ \overline{4}\ \overline{18}$ $\overline{15}\ \overline{7}\ \overline{1}\ \overline{16}$ $\overline{4}\ \overline{18}\ \overline{1}\ \overline{19}$ $\overline{17}\ \overline{7}\ \overline{16}\ \overline{10}$. $\overline{7}$

$\overline{17}\ \overline{1}\ \overline{20}\ \overline{18}\ \overline{14}\ \overline{5}$ $\overline{15}\ \overline{7}\ \overline{21}\ \overline{10}\ \overline{20}\ \overline{3}\ \overline{14}\ \overline{18}\ \overline{5}$ $\overline{2}\ \overline{20}\ \overline{13}$ $\overline{20}\ \overline{17}$ $\overline{10}\ \overline{2}\ \overline{18}$

$\overline{8}\ \overline{3}\ \overline{6}\ \overline{20}\ \overline{15}\ \overline{18}$ $\overline{15}\ \overline{7}\ \overline{21}\ \overline{22}\ \overline{2}\ \overline{10}$ $\overline{2}\ \overline{20}\ \overline{13}$, $\overline{2}\ \overline{20}\ \overline{16}$ $\overline{5}\ \overline{1}\ \overline{20}\ \overline{4}\ \overline{18}\ \overline{1}\ \overline{16}$, $\overline{}$

$\overline{6}\ \overline{20}\ \overline{15}\ \overline{18}\ \overline{14}\ \overline{16}\ \overline{18}$ $\overline{9}\ \overline{3}\ \overline{21}\ \overline{6}\ \overline{5}$ $\overline{23}\ \overline{18}$ $\overline{10}\ \overline{7}\ \overline{11}\ \overline{18}\ \overline{14}$ $\overline{7}\ \overline{9}\ \overline{7}\ \overline{19}$.

$\overline{6}\ \overline{21}\ \overline{15}\ \overline{20}\ \overline{7}\ \overline{14}\ \overline{3}$ $\overline{20}\ \overline{16}$ $\overline{16}\ \overline{7}\ \overline{20}\ \overline{5}$ $\overline{10}\ \overline{3}$ $\overline{2}\ \overline{7}\ \overline{4}\ \overline{18}$

$\overline{1}\ \overline{18}\ \overline{8}\ \overline{6}\ \overline{20}\ \overline{18}\ \overline{5}$,   "$\overline{10}\ \overline{2}\ \overline{18}\ \overline{19}$ $\overline{15}\ \overline{7}\ \overline{14}\ \overline{10}$ $\overline{20}$, $\overline{5}\ \overline{3}\ \overline{14}\ \overline{10}$, $\overline{2}\ \overline{7}\ \overline{4}\ \overline{18}$

$\overline{3}\ \overline{14}\ \overline{18}$!"

CRYPTIC STORY
Luciano Pavarotti

Each story has a message in substitution code. (One letter of the alphabet has been substituted for the correct letter.) When you have discovered one word, use the known letters to help decode other words. Use the clues!

RSTYTATG IGEATVQYL JY EY EQGXVEYT, XEAEGJIIQ ZONU EY TMJYJWN

XGQMTH IQMPTI. ST HJTU YJI ZTVQTAT QY IST CGQAJVJOU "TKIGEU"

QYMVOHTH QY CQGUI MVEUU.

Here are some clues to help you start; *A* is represented by *E*; *E* by *T*; *N* by *Y*; *R* by *G*; *O* by *J*; and *D* by *H*. Good luck!

CHALLENGER CRYPTIC STORY

BYILDGZ VDODKZWWL ZAGX WAZ CZUHX. ZGH LX LG UZSHGD, WCH ILWR

ZM CLX NLKWC DGS NZRCZZS. LG 1974, CH NZYQCW D XHDXLSH CZYXH LG

VHXDKZ, WCH BZOHBR ZBS WZAG ZG WCH DSKLDWLI XHD. GZA LW LX

KHGZODWHS DGS UZSHKGLFHS WZ WCH VDODKZWWL MDULBR GHHSX.

HDIC XYUUHK WCH VDODKZWWLX HXIDVH WZ BZXH WCHUXHBOHX LG

MDULBR BLMH . . . DG LGWHKBYSH WZ KHUHUNHK.

To start you off, here are some clues. *A* is represented by *D*; *E* by *H*; *N* by *G*; *O* by *Z*; and *R* by *K*. Good luck!

ITZHAK PERLMAN

Itzhak Perlman was born on August 31, 1945, in Tel Aviv, Israel. When he was three years old, an old recording of violinist Jascha Heifetz was played many times over the radio. This caught his interest and he demanded a violin; his parents soon bought him one and lessons began. He was stricken with polio in 1949, leaving him permanently crippled in both legs. During his year-long recuperation he continued to develop. Now an internationally recognized virtuoso, he is second to none among the young violinists of today.

NOTABLE TRIVIA

A group of young musicians enjoy themselves professionally and as human beings. Violinist Pinchas Zuckerman, (also a conductor); Zubin Mehta, conductor of the New York Philharmonic, who was born in Bombay, India; Vladimir Ashkenzay, Russian-born pianist; and Daniel Barenboim, Argentine-born conductor of the French National Orchestra, along with Itzhak Perlman jokingly call themselves the ''Jewish Mafia'' or the ''Kosher Nostra'' . . . showing a bit of their irrepressible humor.

ITZHAK PERLMAN
OR
"THE PUCKISH MASTER
OF THE VIOLIN"

```
I N C R E D I B L E S C U R L Y
T I N F L U E N C E D E E Q S T
R D N A L O P R T I C X R U E I
Y S U T N T I S M S T Z B A H L
T T F E O P I R O R Z T A L C A
I I P U P N A L O A O E S I T N
L S R L I W A V J E T F S T U O
A S E L O J E T S L O I T Y R S
T D O I E R O O I O P E R A C R
I I R R T G L K O O C H A D L E
V I R T U O S O E O N H C T I P
```

The eight-letter Mystery Word is a favorite vacation location enjoyed by the Perlmans and their four children.

WORDS TO FIND

Aspen, bass, cares, cook, crippled, crutches, curly, extrovert, fun, Heifetz, incredible, influenced, intonation, Israel, jazz, joke, legs, opera, personality, pitch, platform, Poland, quality, sits, solo, top, tours, trill, try, violinist, virtuoso vitality, warm

71

ITZHAK PERLMAN

Tie the information together. Social studies and music meet in these facts. Discuss, question and encourage reading and research for deeper understanding of the life of those times.

Happenings in His Life

1945—Itzhak Perlman is born on August 31 in Tel Aviv, Israel.

1948—A recording of violinist Jascha Heifetz inspires young Itzhak.

1949—He is stricken with polio.

1967—Itzhak marries Toby Lynn Friedlanger, who is also a violinist, on January 5.

1970—Itzhak teaches at Aspen, Colorado, during the summer; it becomes a favorite place for him and his family.

1983—He appears on NBC TV *Gala* with the New York Philharmonic conducted by Zubin Mehta.

During That Time in the United States

1945—Weather radar is developed.

1948—The long playing record (33⅓) is developed.

1949—It is discovered this year that bees use the sun as a compass.

1967—Lyndon Johnson is President.

1970—Burt Bacharach wins an Academy Award for the song ''Raindrops Keep Falling on My Head.''

1983—Ronald Reagan is President.

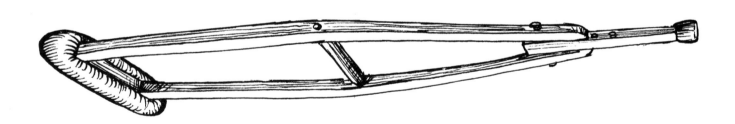

MAKING THE SUBJECT COME ALIVE
(Suggested Activities for Children)
Itzhak Perlman

1. Make a map of Israel. Locate Tel Aviv and Jerusalem.
2. Invite a violinist to play for your class or perhaps a member of the class may be able to perform.
3. Imagine you are a violinist performing before an audience and one of your violin strings breaks.
4. Read about Antonio Stradivarius, violin maker of Cremona, Italy, who lived in the 1600's.
5. Pretend Itzhak Perlman is talking to violinists Thomas Jefferson and Roman Emperor Nero.

NUMBER WORD GAME
Itzhak Perlman

Refer to the story section for answers. Place the letters of your answers on the blanks after the clues. Transfer the letters to the same numbered blanks throughout the paragraph below. A story will result.

1. Give the name of this musician.

     __ __ __ __ __ __   __ __ __ __ __ __ __
     15 20 7 10 8 23   18 14 5 13 11 8 2

2. What is his instrument?

     __ __ __ __ __ __
     21 15 9 13 15 2

3. Whose recording sparked his interest in the violin?

     __ __ __ __ __ __   __ __ __ __ __ __ __
     1 8 16 3 10 8   10 14 15 6 14 20 7

4. He possesses this nonmusical trait in abundance.

     __ __ __ __ __ __ __ __ __ __ __ __ __
     14 12 20 5 8 9 5 22 15 2 8 5 25

     __ __ __ __ __ __ __
     3 9 24 5 8 19 14

5. He and his family like to spend the summer here.

     __ __ __ __ __,   __ __ __ __ __ __ __ __
     8 16 18 14 2   3 9 13 9 5 8 22 9

6. These are two words describing his personality.

     __ __ __ __ __,   __ __ __ __ __ __ __ __ __ __
     4 15 20 20 25   22 14 17 9 2 8 15 5 14

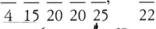

__ __   __   __ __ __ __ __ __ __ __   __ __ __ __ - __ __ __ __,   __ __ 1958,
8 16   8   20 10 15 5 20 14 14 2   25 14 8 5   9 13 22   15 2

__ __ __ __ __ __   __ __ __ __ __ __ __ __   __ __   __ __   " __ __
15 20 7 10 8 23   20 5 8 21 14 13 14 22   9 2   8 2   14 22

__ __ __ __ __ __ __ __   __ __ __ __ __ __ __   __ __   __ __ __ __ __ ,,.
16 24 13 13 15 21 8 2   3 8 5 8 21 8 2   9 6   16 20 8 5 16

__ __ __ .   __ __ __ __ __ __   __ __ __ __ __ __ __ __   __ __ __ __ __ __   __ __ __
20 9 24 5   20 10 15 16   15 16 5 8 14 13 15   2 8 20 15 21 14   8 2 22

__ __ __   __ __ __ __ __ __   __ __ __ __ __   __ __ __ __ __   __ __   __ __ __
10 15 16   6 8 11 15 13 25   13 8 20 14 5   11 9 21 14 22   20 9   2 14 4

__ __ __ __   __ __ __ __ __ .   __ __ __ __ __ __   __ __   __ __ __ __ __ __ __ __ __
25 9 5 23   3 15 20 25   20 10 14 5 14   10 14   3 9 2 20 15 2 24 14 22

__ __ __   __ __ __ __ __ __ __   __ __ __ __ __ __ __ __ __ .
10 15 16   11 24 16 15 3 8 13   14 22 24 3 8 20 15 9 2

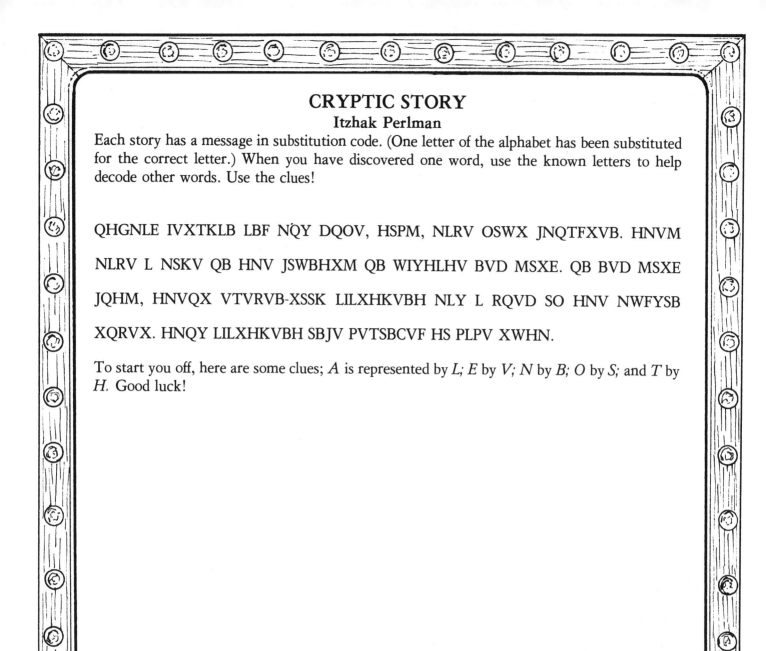

CRYPTIC STORY
Itzhak Perlman

Each story has a message in substitution code. (One letter of the alphabet has been substituted for the correct letter.) When you have discovered one word, use the known letters to help decode other words. Use the clues!

QHGNLE IVXTKLB LBF NQY DQOV, HSPM, NLRV OSWX JNQTFXVB. HNVM

NLRV L NSKV QB HNV JSWBHXM QB WIYHLHV BVD MSXE. QB BVD MSXE

JQHM, HNVQX VTVRVB-XSSK LILXHKVBH NLY L RQVD SO HNV NWFYSB

XQRVX. HNQY LILXHKVBH SBJV PVTSBCVF HS PLPV XWHN.

To start you off, here are some clues; *A* is represented by *L; E* by *V; N* by *B; O* by *S;* and *T* by *H.* Good luck!

CHALLENGER CRYPTIC STORY

ZXBPFK HREML XR MFX. PM ZL F DRTOAMX IRRK. PZL UFLL ERZIM NFL PMFOS

ZY XPM RYM-HZYM CFOX RG F WFZHMO, RY F XE CORSTIXZRY. NZXP

IRYSTIXRO-IRACRLMO FYSOM COMEZY, PM OMIROSMS LRAM RG LIRXX

WRCHZY'L OFDL.

Good luck in this difficult cryptic story! To start you off, here are some of the letters and those they represent . . . *A* is represented by *F; T* by *X; H* by *P; E* by *M* and *O* by *R.*

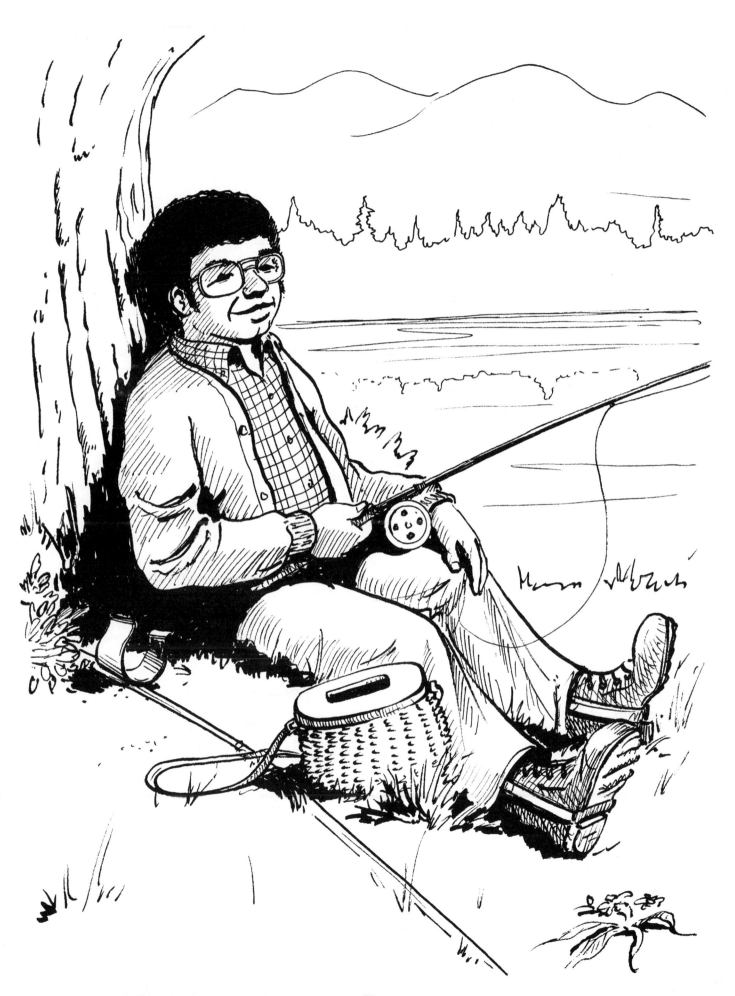

MSTISLAV ROSTROPOVICH

Mstislav Rostropovich was born on March 27, 1927, in Baku, a seaport on the Caspian Sea. It is the capital of the southern province of Azerbaijan in the Soviet Union. He was raised in a musical family; his mother was an accomplished pianist and his father was a distinguished cellist who had studied with Pablo Casals. Mstislav showed musical talent at an early age and played in public when quite young. By the time he was twenty, he was a success in Russia. International appearances soon ranked him with the great cellists of this time. Prokofiev, Shostakovich, Piston and Britten have dedicated works to him which he also performed. He smuggled Shostakovich's *Thirteenth Symphony* (Babi Yar) out of Russia, by removing the title page and substituting an unknown work by an unknown composer. Later, the true title page was replaced. It was first conducted by Eugene Ormandy in the United States in 1970. Rostropovich and his wife were stripped of Soviet citizenship in 1978. In 1981, he was appointed Musical Director of the National Symphony Orchestra in Washington, D.C.

NOTABLE TRIVIA

In 1974, he bought the Duport cello, made by Antonio Stradivarius in 1711. Outside of an interesting scar on the lower part of the body of the cello, it was perfect. Napoleon Bonaparte accidentally made that scar with the spur of his boot, after Duport, a cellist, had played for him and Napoleon had asked to look at the instrument.

MSTISLAV ROSTROPOVICH
OR
"COURAGEOUS OUTSPOKEN CELLIST"

```
D Y N A M I C I T A M O L P I D
E R O C S H O M E S P I R I T C
D R I S K R O W E I O T W O D B
I I D V N D Q N H E A S H E R U
C D R H E U E S E N T E N A D S
A G R E A T N W I K A W Y R R Y
T I R L C E L L O V O I C N A D
E F I P Z T A G A N B P S S W N
D T E I E G O L E A R H S S A A
Y S T X T A S R B E S T I T U M
O I T A L K S M U G G L E D U R
C O N T R O V E R S I A L S E O
```

Mystery Word (nine letters): Two were dedicated to Rostropovich by the Russian composer Dimitri Shostakovich.

WORDS TO FIND

adds, award, Babi Yar, best, busy, cello, citizenship, controversial, dedicated, diplomatic, director, drive, dynamic, earns, freedom, Galina, gifts, goal, great, hard, help, hide, home, meet, Ormandy, outspoken, owed, quality, renowned, risk, Russian, score, Slav, smuggled, spirit, talks, text, two, west, work

MSTISLAV ROSTROPOVICH

Tie the information together. Social studies and music meet in these facts. Discuss, question and encourage reading and research for deeper understanding of the life of those times.

Happenings in His Life

1927—On March 27, Mstislav Rostropovich is born in Baku, now a part of the Soviet Union.

1933—Mstislav enters the Moscow Conservatory of Music.

1953—He becomes a teacher at the Moscow Conservatory of Music.

1956—Rostropovich makes his American debut on April 4 in Carnegie Hall.

1966—Mstislav is awarded the Peoples' Artist of the Soviet Union.

1981—He becomes Musical Director of the National Symphony Orchestra in Washington, D.C.

During That Time in the United States

1927—Calvin Coolidge is President.

1933—During this year FM radio broadcasting is presented to the public.

1953—For the very first time hearing aid transistors are used.

1956—American actress Grace Kelly marries Prince Rainier of Monaco.

1966—A soft landing on the moon is made by American spaceship *Surveyor I.*

1977—Gordie Howe scores 1,000 goals . . . the first man in the history of hockey to achieve that number.

MAKING THE SUBJECT COME ALIVE
(Suggested Activities for Children)
Mstislav Rostropovich

1. Make a map of the Union of Soviet Socialist Republics. Locate the cities of Baku, Moscow and Leningrad.
2. Make a detailed drawing of a cello; name and locate the various parts of this instrument.
3. Invite a cellist to play and demonstrate his instrument for the class.
4. Read about conductors. Why are they necessary? What requirements are needed to be a good one?
5. Interview a professional musician; discuss their views of orchestra conductors.
6. Collect newspaper clippings about Mstislav Rostropovich as a cellist and conductor.

NUMBER WORD GAME
Mstislav Rostropovich

Refer to the story section for answers. Place the letters of your answers on the blanks after the clues. Transfer the letters to the same numbered blanks throughout the paragraph below. A story will result.

1. Name this musician. ___ ___ ___ ___ ___ ___ ___ ___   ___ ___ ___ ___ ___ ___ ___ ___ ___ ___ ___ ___
           3   4 18 5   4 12 10 20   7 14   4 18   7 14 24 14 20   5 21 9

2. Name the city and country where he   ___ ___ ___ ___,   ___ ___ ___ ___ ___ ___
   was born and grew up.   15 10 19 22   7 22   4   4   5 10

3. How his spirits often seem   ___ ___ ___ ___ ___ ___
                          13 14 16 14 22   4

4. What is his instrument?   ___ ___ ___ ___ ___
                   21 11 12 12 14

5. What is one of his many gifts?   ___ ___ ___ ___ ___ ___ ___ ___ ___ ___ ___ ___ ___   ___ ___ ___ ___ ___ ___
                     11 25 18   7 10 14   7   6   5   8 10   7 16   18 10 12 11   8 18

___ ___ ___ ___ ___ ___   ___ ___ ___ ___ ___ ___   ___ ___ ___ ___ ___ ___   " ___ ___ ___ "
1 10   3 14 22   4   24 11 14 24 12 11   24 12 10 16 11   6   18 14 16

___ ___ ___ ___ ___ ___ ___ ___ ___ ___ ___.   ___ ___ ___   ___ ___ ___ ___ ___ ___ ___ ___ ___
5   8   4 18   7 22   3 11   8 18   4   18   9 11   14   7 21   9 11   4 18   7 10

___ ___ ___   ___ ___ ___   ___ ___   ___ ___ ___ ___ ___   ___ ___ ___ ___ ___ ___
17 10   4   12 11   6   15 16   1   7 10   8   2   13 14   4 11 24   9

___ ___ ___ ___ ___   (___ ___ ___ ___ ___   ___ ___ ___ ___ ___ ___ ___ ___ ___ ___ ___)
9 10 16   6   8   10 12   5 10   4   7 14   4 18   7 14 24 14 20   5 21   9

___ ___   " ___ ___ ___   ___ ___ ___   ___ ___ ___ ___ ___ ___ ___ ___."
5   8   18   9 11   18 14 16   4 16   3 24   9 14   8 16

___ ___ ___ ___ ___ ___ ___ ___ ___ ___   ___ ___ ___   ___ ___ ___   ___ ___ ___ ___
22   8 11 25 24 11 21 18 11   6   1 22   8   10   8   6   3 22 21   9

___ ___ ___ ___ ___ ___ ___ ___   ___ ___ ___   ___ ___ ___   ___ ___ ___ ___ ___ ___.
12 10 22 23   9 18 11   7   17 10   4   18   9 11   7 11   4 22 12 18

CRYPTIC STORY

Mstislav Rostropovich

Each story has a message in substitution code. (One letter of the alphabet has been substituted for the correct letter.) When you have discovered one word, use the known letters to help decode other words. Use the clues!

"QOMMGAHOD" SIU MNG VIEG ZFBGV MT I RIVJ-ATBGA BIV EUMFURIB IVJ

ZIRFVI ATUMATDTBFHN QTOZNM FV GVZRIVJ. EUMFURIB PTOVJ I NTAV

MNIM "ETTGJ" RFWG I HTS. MNGK FVUMIRRGJ FM FV MNG RIVJ-ATBGA.

QIHW MT ETUHTS MNGK JATBG, ETTFVZ IRR MNG SIK IHATUU GOATDG,

EOHN MT MNG DOLLRGEGVM TP RTHIR HTSU.

Here are clues to help you. *A* is represented by *I*; *E* by *G*; *N* by *V*; *O* by *T*; and *R* by *A*. Good luck!

CHALLENGER CRYPTIC STORY

YWETWBFQ VFW F ETRH SMD EVFE VFW BMRD EFUUH-NMBMJIS VFTJ. VI

MUEIR KJTRDW VTY EM MJNVIWEJF JIVIFJWFBW GVIR VI TW EVI NIBBM

WMBMTWE. FW JMWEJMXMQTNV XIJUMJYW MR VTW NIBBM, EVI ETRH SMD

WTEW AOTIEBH ORSIJ VTW YFWEIJ'W NVFTJ. VI WIIYW EM JINMDRTCI EVI

UTRFB NFSIRNI, UMJ VI TYYISTFEIBH POYXW OX FRS JORW KIEGIIR EVI JMGW

MU EVI WEJTRD WINETMR, KFJZTRD VFXXTBH FBB EVI ETYI.

Good luck in breaking the code! Here are a few helps to start you off. *A* is represented by *F*; *E* by *I*; *N* by *R*; and *D* by *S*.

ANDRÉS SEGOVIA

Andrés Segovia was born on February 18, 1893, in the Andalusian city of Linares, Spain. He was raised in Granada. His father, a lawyer, hoped he would eventually join him in his law offices. This was not to be. Andrés had violin and piano lessons at an early age. One day he heard a guitar being played and was completely captivated. When his family objected to his study of this instrument, he persisted, and, unable to find a competent teacher, used his musical knowledge and developed his own technique. His use of the right hand involved the use of fingernails and fingertips in a subtly different manner to create a wide range of tone colors and volume, with much less hand movement.

He insisted the guitar had a rightful place on the concert stage. Musicians of that day did not agree with him. Segovia perfected his technique and enlarged the guitar repertoire. He discovered that music written for the lute could be arranged for the Spanish guitar. His transcriptions of some of Bach's music have become concert favorites. His impeccable musicianship and technique created interest in the guitar and brought it from the ''outskirts of music'' to a respected place on the concert stage. It has become one of the most popular instruments for amateurs.

Composers have written guitar concertos and other pieces for Andrés Segovia. Worldwide concerts, recordings, and master classes have made him an unchallenged master of the Spanish guitar.

NOTABLE TRIVIA

He is tall and possesses a quiet charm. He lives quietly with his wife in an Upper East Side apartment in Manhattan, New York.

ANDRÉS SEGOVIA

OR
"ENCHANTED GUITAR . . . MAGIC FINGERS"

```
D Y N A M I C S R D R O F X O
A T E C N E T S I S R E P S B
I E N I U R S E L F T O O S S
M R R A N G E T E F O U L R T
R I W A R E C U E B T O I O A
O O H I T B Q L S R O C T N C
F T A O S I I E H L H O L
S R N T N E U V T N S A G H E
N E D H F I N G E R N A I L S
A P C A R T I S T R Y K R O W
R E Y W A L S S P A N I S H L
T R A N S C R I P T I O N S P
```

The seven-letter Mystery Word, Segovia has given all over the world.

WORDS TO FIND

aim, artistry, color, dynamics, fingernails, foot, globe, guitar, hand, honors, lawyer, left, lute, obstacles, Oxford, persistence, phrases, range, repertoire, richness, right, ruin, self, site, Spanish, technique, tone, transcriptions, transform, vibrant, virtuoso, wise, work

ANDRÉS SEGOVIA

Tie the information together! Social studies and music meet in these facts. Discuss, question and encourage reading and research for deeper understanding of the life of those times.

Happenings in His Life

1893—Andrés Segovia is born in Linares, Spain, on February 18.

1899—Andrés receives his first guitar lesson; he is six years old.

1908—Andrés gives his first guitar recital in Grenada, Spain.

1924—He makes a concert tour of South America.

1932—Italian composer Castelnuovo-Tedesco composes *Concerto in D major* for Segovia.

1977—His last LP recording is made.

1982—Master classes given at the Metropolitan Museum of Art in New York City

During That Time in the United States

1893—Grover Cleveland is President.

1899—The sousaphone is developed; it is a rearranged tuba.

1908—The Lincoln penny replaces the Indian head penny.

1924—Calvin Coolidge is elected President.

1932—This year is the lowest point of the Depression years.

1977—French-built supersonic jet *Concorde* starts flights to New York between Paris and London.

1982—Ronald Reagan is President.

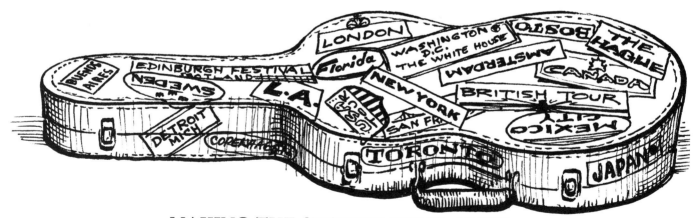

MAKING THE SUBJECT COME ALIVE
(Suggested Activities for Children)
Andrés Segovia

1. Draw a picture of a guitar; label all its parts.
2. Pretend you are carrying your guitar in its case through a crowded store, along a street surging with people and into a very crowded restaurant. Cope with your clumsy instrument case.
3. Invite a guitarist to play for your class.
4. Define ''classical'' guitar, Spanish guitar, electric guitar and know the differences between each one.

NUMBER WORD GAME
Andrés Segovia

Refer to the story section for answers. Place the letters of your answers on the blanks after the clues. Transfer the letters to the same numbered blanks throughout the paragraph below. A story will result.

1. Give this guitar virtuoso's complete name.

$\overline{10}\ \overline{8}\ \overline{4}\ \overline{22}\ \overline{9}\ \overline{14}\quad \overline{14}\ \overline{9}\ \overline{6}\ \overline{2}\ \overline{23}\ \overline{15}\ \overline{10}$

2. Name the town and country of his birth.

$\overline{3}\ \overline{15}\ \overline{8}\ \overline{10}\ \overline{22}\ \overline{9}\ \overline{14},\quad \overline{14}\ \overline{20}\ \overline{10}\ \overline{15}\ \overline{8}$

3. Name one quality he possesses in great abundance.

$\overline{9}\ \overline{12}\ \overline{1}\ \overline{22}\ \overline{10}\ \overline{2}\ \overline{22}\ \overline{4}\ \overline{15}\ \overline{8}\ \overline{10}\ \overline{22}\ \overline{25},$

$\overline{16}\ \overline{10}\ \overline{5}\ \overline{18}\ \overline{3}\ \overline{2}\ \overline{18}\ \overline{14}\quad \overline{1}\ \overline{9}\ \overline{13}\ \overline{17}\ \overline{8}\ \overline{15}\ \overline{7}\ \overline{18}\ \overline{9}$

4. What is his philosophy on long life?   "$\overline{11}\ \overline{2}\ \overline{22}\ \overline{21}\quad \overline{11}\ \overline{17}\ \overline{9}\ \overline{8}\quad \overline{11}\ \overline{10}\ \overline{1}\ \overline{9}\ \overline{22}$

$\overline{15}\ \overline{14}\quad \overline{14}\ \overline{1}\ \overline{15}\ \overline{3}\ \overline{3},\quad \overline{15}\ \overline{1}\quad \overline{5}\ \overline{9}\ \overline{13}\ \overline{2}\ \overline{24}\ \overline{9}\ \overline{14}\quad \overline{14}\ \overline{1}\ \overline{10}\ \overline{6}\ \overline{8}\ \overline{10}\ \overline{8}\ \overline{1}."

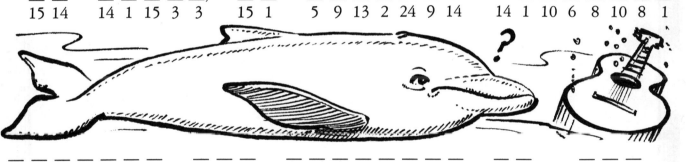

$\overline{14}\ \overline{9}\ \overline{6}\ \overline{2}\ \overline{23}\ \overline{15}\ \overline{10}\quad \overline{11}\ \overline{10}\ \overline{14}\quad \overline{14}\ \overline{11}\ \overline{15}\ \overline{24}\ \overline{24}\ \overline{15}\ \overline{8}\ \overline{6}\quad \overline{15}\ \overline{8}\quad \overline{1}\ \overline{17}\ \overline{9}$

$\overline{24}\ \overline{9}\ \overline{4}\ \overline{15}\ \overline{1}\ \overline{9}\ \overline{22}\ \overline{22}\ \overline{10}\ \overline{8}\ \overline{9}\ \overline{10}\ \overline{8}\quad \overline{14}\ \overline{9}\ \overline{10}\quad \overline{11}\ \overline{17}\ \overline{9}\ \overline{8}\quad \overline{17}\ \overline{9}$

$\overline{5}\ \overline{9}\ \overline{13}\ \overline{10}\ \overline{24}\ \overline{9}\quad \overline{10}\ \overline{11}\ \overline{10}\ \overline{22}\ \overline{9}\quad \overline{2}\ \overline{16}\quad \overline{10}\quad \overline{17}\ \overline{18}\ \overline{6}\ \overline{9}\quad \overline{14}\ \overline{17}\ \overline{10}\ \overline{4}\ \overline{2}\ \overline{11}$

$\overline{16}\ \overline{2}\ \overline{3}\ \overline{3}\ \overline{2}\ \overline{11}\ \overline{15}\ \overline{8}\ \overline{6}\quad \overline{17}\ \overline{15}\ \overline{24}\quad \overline{10}\quad \overline{14}\ \overline{17}\ \overline{10}\ \overline{22}\ \overline{21}!\quad \overline{10}\quad \overline{24}\ \overline{2}\ \overline{1}\ \overline{2}\ \overline{22}$

$\overline{5}\ \overline{2}\ \overline{10}\ \overline{1}\quad \overline{11}\ \overline{10}\ \overline{14}\quad \overline{14}\ \overline{9}\ \overline{8}\ \overline{1}\quad \overline{1}\ \overline{2}\quad \overline{22}\ \overline{9}\ \overline{14}\ \overline{13}\ \overline{18}\ \overline{9}\quad \overline{17}\ \overline{15}\ \overline{24}.$

$\overline{16}\ \overline{15}\ \overline{8}\ \overline{10}\ \overline{3}\ \overline{3}\ \overline{25},\quad \overline{10}\ \overline{1}\quad \overline{1}\ \overline{17}\ \overline{9}\quad \overline{5}\ \overline{2}\ \overline{10}\ \overline{1},\quad \overline{10}\quad \overline{22}\ \overline{9}\ \overline{10}\ \overline{14}\ \overline{14}\ \overline{18}\ \overline{22}\ \overline{15}\ \overline{8}\ \overline{6}$

$\overline{23}\ \overline{2}\ \overline{15}\ \overline{13}\ \overline{9}\quad \overline{13}\ \overline{10}\ \overline{3}\ \overline{3}\ \overline{9}\ \overline{4},\quad "\overline{15}\ \overline{1}\ \overline{14}\quad \overline{10}\quad \overline{4}\ \overline{2}\ \overline{3}\ \overline{20}\ \overline{17}\ \overline{15}\ \overline{8}$

$\overline{5}\ \overline{9}\ \overline{15}\ \overline{8}\ \overline{6}\quad \overline{16}\ \overline{22}\ \overline{15}\ \overline{9}\ \overline{8}\ \overline{4}\ \overline{3}\ \overline{25}!"\quad \overline{11}\ \overline{17}\ \overline{10}\ \overline{1}\quad \overline{10}\quad \overline{22}\ \overline{9}\ \overline{3}\ \overline{15}\ \overline{9}\ \overline{16}!$

85

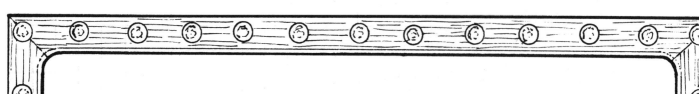

CRYPTIC STORY
Andrés Segovia

Each story has a message in substitution code. (One letter of the alphabet has been substituted for the correct letter.) When you have discovered one word, use the known letters to help decode other words. Use the clues!

WRO PBAQW TUKTOAWU PUA JZBWEA TUXFUQOL BK WRO WMOKWBOWR

TOKWZAI MEQ MABWWOK GI BWEYBEK TUXFUQOA XEABU TEQWOYKZUHU-

WOLOQTU PUA QOJUHBE. WRO TUKTOAWU BK L XENUA REQ GOOK LO-

QTABGOL EQ ''GBWWOAQMOOW.''

Here are some helps to get you started in this Cryptic Story. *A* is represented by *E; D* by *L; C* by *T; H* by *R;* and *T* by *W.* Good luck!

CHALLENGER CRYPTIC STORY

FVVEKYHL REAAHWYV JM VHOECTF . . . ''YDH VEXWL EZ YDH OXTYFK EW

KHREKL LEHV WEY DFCH YDH LHSTRFRM, YDH UEHYKM, FWL WXFWRH

UKHVHWY TW YDH TWVYKXAHWY'V STCH VEXWL.'' . . . ''YDH HSHRYKTR

OXTYFK KEJV YDH OXTYFK EZ TYV UEHYKM FWL LHSTRTEXV VEXWL.'' . . .

FJEXY YELFM'V FCFWY-OFKLH PKTYTWO . . . ''YDHM PKTYH UTHRHV PTYD

VEXWLV . . . EEU, HHHU, FDDD . . . FWL RFSS YDFY AXVTR. TY TV WEY.''

Good luck in decoding! Here are some letters and those representing them. *E* is represented by *H; H* by *D; N* by *W; S* by *V* and *R* by *K.*

BEVERLY SILLS

Beverly Sills was born on May 25, 1929, in Brooklyn, New York. In those days her name was Belle Miriam Silverman. She was a very young radio performer, starting when she was three years old. Very interested in music, at seven years of age she had learned many arias by listening to her mother's recordings of Galli-Curci. It was not until she was twelve years old that she started studying music seriously.

In 1946, she made her debut with the Philadelphia Civic Opera Company. With her debut at the New York City Opera in 1955, an award-filled career started soaring to new heights. She appeared at La Scala Opera House in Milan, Italy, in 1969 and Covent Garden in London, England, in 1970. Finally, in 1975, she made her first appearance at the Metropolitan Opera in New York City.

This red-haired beauty has appeared in many TV specials, *Galas,* and *Live from Lincoln Center.* At present she is Administrator and General Director of the New York City Opera.

Beverly Sills, American lyric coloratura soprano has received five Honorary Doctor's Degrees!

NOTABLE TRIVIA

As a child, her mother gave her naturally blonde hair an extra blonde rinse. Later on, a hairdresser did not mix the rinse correctly and her hair came out an interesting red. Everyone liked it . . . so it is today!

BEVERLY SILLS OR "SING, . . . YOU BUBBLING BEAUTY!"

```
S O P R A N O H H I G H T I W
N T D I S C I P L I N E D O E
N R A N O I T A V O P E R A U
Y S A G N I S E H E R K E N Q
L A M E E E S T V P A T I A I
K I E S L C A A W I M Q N R N
O R T B E E R E D A U U T O H
O A B B R N J A R E D R I E C
R U A B O Y O R F E N C O R E
B E V E R L Y T K T N E L A T
```

The ten-letter Mystery Word is something this artist has experienced in abundance.

WORDS TO FIND

Aida, arias, Beverly, boy, breath, Brooklyn, Bubbles, control, discipline, do, encore, gives, high, Jew, joy, learn, marry, met, opera, ovation, rave, red, soprano, sing, stagecraft, talent, technique, tones, triumph, wit, work, unique

BEVERLY SILLS

Tie the information together! Social studies and music meet in these facts. Discuss, question and encourage reading and research for deeper understanding of the life of those times.

Happenings in Her Life	During That Time in the United States
1929—Belle Miriam Silverman (Beverly Sills) is born on May 25.	1929—Frozen foods are first introduced by Charles Birdseye.
1936—At 7 years of age, she has learned 22 operatic arias by listening to records.	1936—The Baseball Hall of Fame is established at Cooperstown, New York.
1955—She makes her debut at the New York City Opera.	1955—Kermit the Frog is created by Jim Henson. Kermit is the first of the Muppets.
1975—Beverly makes her first appearance at the Metropolitan Opera in New York City.	1975—Hockey's Stanley Cup is won by the Philadelphia Flyers.
1979—On July 1, she becomes the Administrator and General Director of the New York City Opera.	1979—A coin found in Bar Harbor, Maine, is the first datable Viking artifact found in North America.

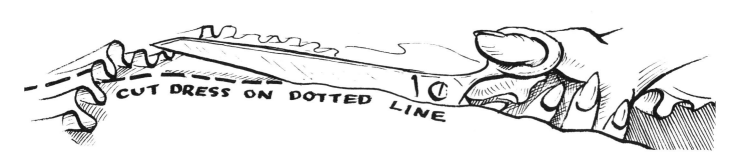

CUT DRESS ON DOTTED LINE

MAKING THE SUBJECT COME ALIVE
(Suggested Activities for Children)
Beverly Sills

1. Frequently Beverly Sills is the hostess on TV *Galas*. Check the TV schedule and watch one to see how she appears in person.
2. Define opera, aria, soprano, lyric, coloratura.
3. Read about her life and make a report to the class. Be sure to use pictures and any other illustrations you may find.
4. Write to her requesting her picture and autograph. (Director, New York City Opera Company, New York State Theater, Lincoln Center.) She would probably appreciate a letter from you.

NUMBER WORD GAME
Beverly Sills

Refer to the story section for answers. Place the letters of your answers on the blanks after the clues. Transfer the letters to the same numbered blanks throughout the paragraph below. A story will result.

1. What is Belle Miriam Silverman's professional name?

   $\overline{17}\ \overline{6}\ \overline{7}\ \overline{6}\ \overline{16}\ \overline{4}\ \overline{1}$ $\overline{19}\ \overline{15}\ \overline{4}\ \overline{4}\ \overline{19}$

2. How is her voice classified?

   $\overline{9}\ \overline{5}\ \overline{4}\ \overline{5}\ \overline{16}\ \overline{20}\ \overline{11}\ \overline{14}\ \overline{16}\ \overline{20}$ $\overline{19}\ \overline{5}\ \overline{2}\ \overline{16}\ \overline{20}\ \overline{3}\ \overline{5}$

3. What is the city and state of her birth?

   $\overline{17}\ \overline{16}\ \overline{5}\ \overline{5}\ \overline{23}\ \overline{4}\ \overline{1}\ \overline{3}$, $\overline{3}\ \overline{6}\ \overline{8}$ $\overline{1}\ \overline{5}\ \overline{16}\ \overline{23}$

4. How have colleges and universities honored her?

   $\overline{25}\ \overline{15}\ \overline{7}\ \overline{6}$ $\overline{13}\ \overline{15}\ \overline{25}\ \overline{25}\ \overline{6}\ \overline{16}\ \overline{6}\ \overline{3}\ \overline{11}$

   $\overline{14}\ \overline{3}\ \overline{15}\ \overline{7}\ \overline{6}\ \overline{16}\ \overline{19}\ \overline{15}\ \overline{11}\ \overline{15}\ \overline{6}\ \overline{19}$ $\overline{18}\ \overline{20}\ \overline{7}\ \overline{6}$ $\overline{10}\ \overline{6}\ \overline{16}$ $\overline{20}\ \overline{3}$

   $\overline{10}\ \overline{5}\ \overline{3}\ \overline{5}\ \overline{16}\ \overline{20}\ \overline{16}\ \overline{1}$ $\overline{13}\ \overline{5}\ \overline{9}\ \overline{11}\ \overline{5}\ \overline{16}\ \overline{19}$ $\overline{13}\ \overline{6}\ \overline{18}\ \overline{16}\ \overline{6}\ \overline{6}$.

5. These words describe the general spirit she presents.

   $\overline{22}\ \overline{5}\ \overline{1}\ \overline{5}\ \overline{14}\ \overline{19}$, $\overline{17}\ \overline{14}\ \overline{17}\ \overline{17}\ \overline{4}\ \overline{15}\ \overline{3}\ \overline{18}$,

   $\overline{10}\ \overline{20}\ \overline{2}\ \overline{2}\ \overline{15}\ \overline{3}\ \overline{6}\ \overline{19}\ \overline{19}$

$\overline{11}\ \overline{10}\ \overline{6}\ \overline{16}\ \overline{6}$ $\overline{20}\ \overline{16}\ \overline{6}$ $\overline{7}\ \overline{20}\ \overline{16}\ \overline{15}\ \overline{5}\ \overline{14}\ \overline{19}$ $\overline{11}\ \overline{1}\ \overline{2}\ \overline{6}\ \overline{19}$ $\overline{5}\ \overline{25}$

$\overline{19}\ \overline{5}\ \overline{2}\ \overline{16}\ \overline{20}\ \overline{3}\ \overline{5}$ $\overline{7}\ \overline{5}\ \overline{15}\ \overline{9}\ \overline{6}\ \overline{19}$. $\overline{11}\ \overline{10}\ \overline{6}$

$\overline{9}\ \overline{5}\ \overline{4}\ \overline{5}\ \overline{16}\ \overline{20}\ \overline{11}\ \overline{14}\ \overline{16}\ \overline{20}$ $\overline{7}\ \overline{5}\ \overline{15}\ \overline{9}\ \overline{6}$ $\overline{15}\ \overline{19}$ $\overline{20}$ $\overline{10}\ \overline{15}\ \overline{18}\ \overline{10}$

$\overline{9}\ \overline{4}\ \overline{6}\ \overline{20}\ \overline{16}$ $\overline{7}\ \overline{5}\ \overline{15}\ \overline{9}\ \overline{6}$ $\overline{9}\ \overline{20}\ \overline{2}\ \overline{20}\ \overline{17}\ \overline{4}\ \overline{6}$ $\overline{5}\ \overline{25}$

$\overline{2}\ \overline{16}\ \overline{5}\ \overline{13}\ \overline{14}\ \overline{9}\ \overline{15}\ \overline{3}\ \overline{18}$ $\overline{20}\ \overline{4}\ \overline{4}$ $\overline{19}\ \overline{5}\ \overline{16}\ \overline{11}\ \overline{19}$ $\overline{5}\ \overline{25}$ $\overline{11}\ \overline{16}\ \overline{15}\ \overline{4}\ \overline{4}\ \overline{19}$

$\overline{20}\ \overline{3}\ \overline{13}$ $\overline{25}\ \overline{20}\ \overline{3}\ \overline{9}\ \overline{1}$ $\overline{5}\ \overline{16}\ \overline{3}\ \overline{20}\ \overline{21}\ \overline{6}\ \overline{3}\ \overline{11}\ \overline{20}\ \overline{4}$ $\overline{3}\ \overline{5}\ \overline{11}\ \overline{6}\ \overline{19}$.

CRYPTIC STORY
Beverly Sills

Each story has a message in substitution code. (One letter of the alphabet has been substituted for the correct letter.) When you have discovered one word, use the known letters to help decode other words. Use the clues!

HPQ VQNWTNXDFJQ ADZ ETSFE AQOO DZ RQKQNOI ZDFE RQDYHSWYOOI,

JDNNISFE D ZXDOO LTE SF PQN DNXZ. ZYLLQFOI, ZPQ RQJDXQ DADNQ TW

ZTXQHPSFE ADNX DFL KQNI AQH ZVNQDLSFE WNTX HPQ LTE; ZPQ

SXXQLSDHQOI VYH PSX LTAF. PQ RQEDF HT PTAO DFL PQN ZTOT RQJDXQ D

LYQH WTN HPQ NQXDSFLQN TW PQN DNSD. HPQ DYLSQFJQ OTKQL HPQ

YFQMVQJHQL DJHSTF.

Here are some clues to start you off. *A* is represented by *D; E* by *Q; N* by *F; O* by *T;* and *T* by *H.* Good luck!

CHALLENGER CRYPTIC STORY

DO VD GSDVD ATCYD NAXGC, LCFCYVM YCUXCGOCJ D SAGOXHC YCHDJC

WZ GWVFCY IAY D YAVC GNC PDG OA GWZR. ONC HDZDRCHCZO GDWJ

''MCG.'' ZAONWZR NDTTCZCJ. DZAONCY YCUXCGO . . . ZAONWZR

NDTTCZCJ. GOWVV DZAONCY YCUXCGO . . . GOWVV ZAONWZR. IWZDVVM,

GNC IAVJCJ ONC SAGOXHC ZCDOVM, OAAQ GSWGGAYG DZJ SDYCIXVVM

SXO WO WZ NDVI. GNC RAO NCY SAGOXHC WZ GWVFCY.

Here are some clues to get you started. *A* is represented by *D; E* by *C; N* by *Z; O* by *A;* and *S* by *G.* Good luck!

92

JOAN SUTHERLAND

Joan Sutherland was born on November 6, 1926, in Sydney, Australia. Her father had a very successful tailoring business. Her mother, who recognized her musical talent and naturally lovely voice, gave her piano and voice lessons. At twenty years of age, she won the first of many scholarships. Eventually one led to study at the Royal Conservatory of Music in London, England. She was accompanied on the piano during her voice lessons by Richard Bonynge, a fellow Australian. Romance blossomed and they were married in 1954. They have one son. Her beautifully sung trills and astounding breath control, as well as the ease in reaching high notes, caused her husband to encourage her in the bel canto style of singing. (Bel canto is Italian for ''beautiful singing.'') This type of vocal technique of eighteenth century Italy stresses beauty of sound and brilliancy of performance rather than expression and emotion. It uses many fancy embellishments and requires a very special type of voice. Joan's singing of the role of Lucia in the opera *Lucia di Lammermoor* made her an international operatic star. All this was achieved through years of hard work.

She is tall and large-boned with a ready smile and an unassuming nature. She was honored in England by being made Dame Commander in the Order of the British Empire in 1979.

NOTABLE TRIVIA
In 1961, she received $7,000 for singing one aria in a TV production.

JOAN SUTHERLAND
OR
"HOW DID YOU GET UP THERE?"

```
N A T U R A L G L O R I O U S
O O A S O U N D A E O B O Y T
D D R A E E Z I S C O T D O A
N Y E M D D L I G R I N N N G
O T P W A A O N N S E E I A E
L I O R R P I M P Y L M C R C
U L I T H G I E H R A L U T R
C A S R N W O R K T I P I I A
I U O I F O C U S E D M N R F
A Q S O L O B R I L L I A N T
```

The seven-letter Mystery Word is important in Joan Sutherland's singing.

WORDS TO FIND

aria, Australia, born, boy, brilliant, canto, ear, focused, glorious, height, London, Lucia, modest, natural, Norma, opera, poise, prima, pure, quality, scot, singing, size, solo, sound, stagecraft, stamina, Sydney, tone, trills, trio, wed, work

JOAN SUTHERLAND

Tie the information together! Social studies and music meet in these facts. Discuss, question and encourage reading and research for deeper understanding of the life of those times.

Happenings in Her Life

1926, November 6—Joan Sutherland is born.

1954—Joan marries English conductor Richard Bonynge.

1961—She is paid $7,000 for singing one aria on a TV program.

1979—She is honored in England by being awarded the CBE by Queen Elizabeth.

During That Time in the United States

1926—Richard E. Byrd with Floyd Bennett make the first successful plane flight over the North Pole.

1954—The *Nautilus*, the first nuclear-powered submarine is launched.

1961—Alan Shepherd is America's first man in space aboard *Freedom 7*.

1979—Pete Rose of Philadelphia Phillies is all-time hitter in National League singles with 2,427.

MAKING THE SUBJECT COME ALIVE
(Suggested Activities for Children)
Joan Sutherland

1. Try to discover how an Australian accent is different from English spoken in America, and English spoken in England.
2. Listen to a recording of Joan Sutherland; notice how all Australian accents are absent.
3. Contrast bel canto singing with regular singing.
4. Make a poster using pictures, newspaper articles, magazine articles or information wherever you may be able to find it.

NUMBER WORD GAME
Joan Sutherland

Refer to the story section for answers. Place the letters of your answers on the blanks after the clues. Transfer the letters to the same numbered blanks throughout the paragraph below. A story will result.

1. Name this famous soprano.
$\overline{7}\ \overline{25}\ \overline{9}\ \overline{6}\quad \overline{19}\ \overline{11}\ \overline{22}\ \overline{14}\ \overline{26}\ \overline{8}\ \overline{3}\ \overline{9}\ \overline{6}\ \overline{16}$

2. Give the city and country of her birth.
$\overline{19}\ \overline{23}\ \overline{16}\ \overline{6}\ \overline{26}\ \overline{23},\quad \overline{9}\ \overline{11}\ \overline{19}\ \overline{22}\ \overline{8}\ \overline{9}\ \overline{3}\ \overline{12}\ \overline{9},$

3. She received a scholarship to this place. Give name and location.
$\overline{8}\ \overline{25}\ \overline{23}\ \overline{9}\ \overline{3}\quad \overline{4}\ \overline{25}\ \overline{6}\ \overline{19}\ \overline{26}\ \overline{8}\ \overline{15}\ \overline{9}\ \overline{22}\ \overline{25}\ \overline{8}$

$\overline{25}\ \overline{18}\quad \overline{10}\ \overline{11}\ \overline{19}\ \overline{12}\ \overline{4},\quad \overline{3}\ \overline{25}\ \overline{6}\ \overline{16}\ \overline{25}\ \overline{6},\quad \overline{26}\ \overline{6}\ \overline{1}\ \overline{3}\ \overline{9}\ \overline{6}$

4. Who is the Australian man she met and married?
$\overline{8}\ \overline{12}\ \overline{4}\ \overline{14}\ \overline{9}\ \overline{8}\ \overline{16}\quad \overline{20}\ \overline{25}\ \overline{6}\ \overline{23}\ \overline{6}\ \overline{1}\ \overline{26}$

5. She is famous for this.
$\overline{15}\ \overline{25}\ \overline{4}\ \overline{9}\ \overline{3}\quad \overline{22}\ \overline{26}\ \overline{4}\ \overline{14}\ \overline{6}\ \overline{12}\ \overline{2}\ \overline{11}\ \overline{26}$

$\overline{7}\ \overline{25}\ \overline{9}\ \overline{6}\quad \overline{19}\ \overline{11}\ \overline{22}\ \overline{14}\ \overline{26}\ \overline{8}\ \overline{3}\ \overline{9}\ \overline{6}\ \overline{16}\quad \overline{12}\ \overline{19}\quad \overline{22}\ \overline{9}\ \overline{3}\ \overline{3}\ \overline{26}\ \overline{8}$

$\overline{22}\ \overline{14}\ \overline{9}\ \overline{6}\quad \overline{10}\ \overline{9}\ \overline{6}\ \overline{23}\quad \overline{25}\ \overline{17}\ \overline{26}\ \overline{8}\ \overline{9}\ \overline{22}\ \overline{12}\ \overline{4}$

$\overline{14}\ \overline{26}\ \overline{8}\ \overline{25}\ \overline{12}\ \overline{6}\ \overline{26}\ \overline{19}.\quad \overline{19}\ \overline{14}\ \overline{26}\quad \overline{12}\ \overline{19}$

$\overline{14}\ \overline{11}\ \overline{10}\ \overline{9}\ \overline{6}\quad \overline{9}\ \overline{6}\ \overline{16}\quad \overline{16}\ \overline{25}\ \overline{26}\ \overline{19}\quad \overline{3}\ \overline{12}\ \overline{24}\ \overline{26}\quad \overline{22}\ \overline{25}\quad \overline{20}\ \overline{26}$

$\overline{4}\ \overline{25}\ \overline{10}\ \overline{18}\ \overline{25}\ \overline{8}\ \overline{22}\ \overline{9}\ \overline{20}\ \overline{3}\ \overline{26}.\quad \overline{19}\ \overline{14}\ \overline{26}\quad \overline{26}\ \overline{6}\ \overline{7}\ \overline{25}\ \overline{23}\ \overline{19}\quad \overline{14}\ \overline{9}\ \overline{15}\ \overline{12}\ \overline{6}$

$\overline{14}\ \overline{26}\ \overline{8}\quad \overline{19}\ \overline{14}\ \overline{25}\ \overline{26}\ \overline{19}\quad \overline{25}\ \overline{18}\ \overline{18}.$

97

CRYPTIC STORY
Joan Sutherland

Each story has a message in substitution code. (One letter of the alphabet has been substituted for the correct letter.) When you have discovered one word, use the known letters to help decode other words. Use the clues!

ZRFUYTYP KVE HV BFZZ TO VYR VB HKR HRMKYTSXRO VB OHFPRMUFBH.

OKR ZRFUYRW UFATWZI. HKRY, ETHK TGATOK WRZTPKH, HKTO OHFHRZI

ZFWI EVXZW JRMVGR XHHRUZI ZTGA FYW MUFOK JFMQEFUWO VY HKR

BZVVU.

Note: To help you in this Cryptic Story, here are some letters and what they represent. Good luck in decoding! *A* is represented by *F;* *E* by *R;* *N* by *Y;* *D* by *W;* and *R* by *U.*

CHALLENGER CRYPTIC STORY

VXFP IGNBSUTFPL AQTT XPTJ IQPM QK BSU BGIDFPL, UQYBFUL DXPJPMS,

YXPLGYNI NBS XUYBSINUF. BQI AQIS FLZQYS BFI MGQLSL NBSQU AXUR

NXMSNBSU KXU NBQUNJ-NBUSS JSFUI. NBSJ BFZS F BXCS QP CXPNUSGO,

IAQNHSUTFPL, YFTTSL ''TSI FZFPNI.''

Here are some clues to help you get started; *A* is represented by *F;* *E* by *S;* *G* by *M;* and *H* by *B.*

Annie
Fiddler on the Roof
The Music Man
My Fair Lady
The Sound of Music

ANNIE

Annie opened on April 21, 1977, at the Alvin Theater in New York City. It was suggested by Harold Grey's comic strip about Annie, red-haired orphan, Sandy, a dog, and Oliver Warbucks, a bald-headed millionaire. Martin Charnin and Charles Strouse created catchy, optimistic and often impish songs.

Annie, an abandoned child, is one of a group of ragamuffins in a Municipal Orphanage Annex for Girls. It is run by a Miss Hannigan, a funny villainous lady who likes to take a drink from a bottle that always seems to be within reach. Famous people like J. Edgar Hoover and Franklin D. Roosevelt enter the story through the magical influence of rich Daddy Warbucks. This is a sentimental look into the past enlivened by the antics of the orphans and Annie's creative problem-solving ideas.

Some favorite songs from this musical are "Tomorrow," "It's a Hard-Knock Life," "Easy Street" and "I Don't Need Anything But You."

NOTABLE TRIVIA
Chicken pox made an appearance in the cast and one after another of the "orphans" came down with this childhood disease. What problems arose!

ANNIE
OR
"OPTIMISM PERSONIFIED"

```
R O O S E V E L T P O D A E O
P I U O Y R D N U A L G D L R
R H C S F I A W D A I G O A P
E C A H S N O E A R A S D E H
S E O M N R E Y L R E A F R A
I I I M R F D S D T B A L D N
D L E O I N G D O D T U M N N
E A M L A C U A G H A I C A I
N O I S S E R P E D N D L K E
T O G E T H E R E N O E M O S
```

The eight-letter Mystery Word is a villainous person who created many problems for Annie.

WORDS TO FIND

adopt, Andrea, Annie, bad, bald, comic, daddy, Depression, dog, dream, duet, easy, Edgar, father, girls, laundry, life, little, mean, orphan, President, rich, Roosevelt, Sandy, smile, solo, someone, together, tomorrow, waifs, Warbucks, you

ANNIE

Tie the information together! Social studies and music meet in these facts. Discuss, question and encourage reading and research for deeper understanding of the life of those times.

Happenings Concerning This Musical

1977—The musical *Annie* opens at the Alvin Theater in New York City on April 21, 1977.

1983—*Annie* closes on January 2, 1983, after giving 2,377 performances.

During That Time in the United States

1977—The United States' space shuttle, *Enterprise* has a successful flight.

1983—Ronald Reagan is President.

MAKING THE SUBJECT COME ALIVE
(Suggested Activities for Children)
Annie

1. Interview a police officer. Ask him how one would search for lost parents. Report your interview to the class.
2. Develop a chorus and sing the songs from *Annie* that you like. Listen to a recording from this musical if you have not heard all of the songs.
3. Create your own dance in the chorus line style; have six girls all dressed in ''ragamuffin'' style.

NUMBER WORD GAME
Annie

Refer back to the story section to find the answers. Place letters of your answers on the blanks after the clues. Transfer the letters to the same numbered blanks throughout the paragraph below. A story will result.

1. Name the heroine and her faithful dog. $\overline{14}\ \overline{2}\ \overline{2}\ \overline{18}\ \overline{19}$, $\overline{21}\ \overline{14}\ \overline{2}\ \overline{1}\ \overline{3}$

2. Name her adopted father. $\overline{1}\ \overline{14}\ \overline{1}\ \overline{1}\ \overline{3}$ $\overline{11}\ \overline{14}\ \overline{4}\ \overline{16}\ \overline{8}\ \overline{10}\ \overline{22}\ \overline{21}$

3. What was his financial status? $\overline{17}\ \overline{18}\ \overline{5}\ \overline{5}\ \overline{18}\ \overline{12}\ \overline{2}\ \overline{14}\ \overline{18}\ \overline{4}\ \overline{19}$

4. Words describing her $\overline{16}\ \overline{4}\ \overline{14}\ \overline{13}\ \overline{19}$, $\overline{12}\ \overline{6}\ \overline{15}\ \overline{18}\ \overline{17}\ \overline{18}\ \overline{21}\ \overline{15}\ \overline{18}\ \overline{10}$

$\overline{14}$ $\overline{15}\ \overline{23}\ \overline{18}\ \overline{4}\ \overline{15}\ \overline{19}\ \overline{19}\ \overline{2}$ $\overline{3}\ \overline{19}\ \overline{14}\ \overline{4}$ $\overline{12}\ \overline{5}\ \overline{1}$ $\overline{11}\ \overline{14}\ \overline{21}$ $\overline{15}\ \overline{23}\ \overline{19}$

$\overline{7}\ \overline{18}\ \overline{4}\ \overline{21}\ \overline{15}$ "$\overline{14}\ \overline{2}\ \overline{2}\ \overline{18}\ \overline{19}$," $\overline{14}\ \overline{2}\ \overline{1}\ \overline{4}\ \overline{19}\ \overline{14}$

$\overline{17}\ \overline{10}\ \overline{14}\ \overline{4}\ \overline{1}\ \overline{5}\ \overline{19}\ \overline{21}$, $\overline{16}\ \overline{5}\ \overline{8}\ \overline{19}\ \overline{20}\ \overline{4}\ \overline{14}\ \overline{3}$ $\overline{19}\ \overline{3}\ \overline{19}\ \overline{21}$

$\overline{21}\ \overline{23}\ \overline{18}\ \overline{2}\ \overline{19}\ \overline{1}$ $\overline{14}\ \overline{21}$ $\overline{21}\ \overline{23}\ \overline{19}$ $\overline{17}\ \overline{14}\ \overline{1}\ \overline{19}$ $\overline{23}\ \overline{19}\ \overline{4}$

$\overline{14}\ \overline{10}\ \overline{15}\ \overline{18}\ \overline{2}\ \overline{20}$ $\overline{1}\ \overline{19}\ \overline{16}\ \overline{8}\ \overline{15}$ $\overline{15}\ \overline{23}\ \overline{19}$ $\overline{12}\ \overline{4}\ \overline{6}\ \overline{23}\ \overline{14}\ \overline{2}\ \overline{21}$

$\overline{14}\ \overline{2}\ \overline{1}$ $\overline{14}\ \overline{2}\ \overline{2}\ \overline{18}\ \overline{19}$ $\overline{23}\ \overline{14}\ \overline{1}$ $\overline{15}\ \overline{12}$ $\overline{16}\ \overline{19}$

$\overline{4}\ \overline{19}\ \overline{6}\ \overline{5}\ \overline{14}\ \overline{10}\ \overline{19}\ \overline{1}$ $\overline{14}\ \overline{21}$ $\overline{15}\ \overline{23}\ \overline{19}\ \overline{3}$ $\overline{20}\ \overline{4}\ \overline{19}\ \overline{11}$ $\overline{8}\ \overline{6}$.

CRYPTIC STORY
Annie

Each story has a message in substitution code. (One letter of the alphabet has been substituted for the correct letter.) When you have discovered one word, use the known letters to help decode other words. Use the clues!

PTDXBQDXP WNTIVXDP GQBM CJQDCVP CNQPX. BMX LTA WVCKQJA

''PCJLK'' NCJ CGCK; RTJPBXNJCBQTJ CJL RTJSYPQTJ NXQAJXL. SQJCVVK, MX

NXBYNJXL TJ MQP TGJ.

Here are some letters to get you started. *A* is represented by *C; D* by *L; E* by *X; N* by *J;* and *R* by *N.* Good luck!

CHALLENGER CRYPTIC STORY

IAL UQXXLC TLJYCL ''PBBSL'' PWWLPCLO YB TCYPOKPM, UPBOM PWWLPCLO

SB IAL FYBBLFISFQI DLCUSYB. AL OSO JYRRYK IAL OSCLFIYC'U UQZZLUISYBU

. . . XYUI YJ IAL ISXL. SB YBL UFLBL PBBSL PBO UPBOM KLCL IY TL FAPULO YJJ

IAL UIPZL TM WYRSFL. UPBOM FAPBZLO IAL PFISYB TM FAPUSBZ IAL WYRSFL

YJJ IAL UIPZL . . . BYI YBFL TQI JYC ULDLCPR WLCJYCXPBFLU.

Here are some clues to help you get started. *A* is represented by *P; E* by *L; N* by *B; O* by *Y; S* by *U.* Good luck!

FIDDLER ON THE ROOF

Fiddler on the Roof opened on September 22, 1964, at the Imperial Theater in New York City. It caught the imagination of the country and became a hit. The music by Jerry Bock and Sheldon Harnick caught the sometimes tragic, sometimes bittersweet events in a haunting manner. Based upon the stories of Jewish writer Sholom Aleichem, this comedy portrays the day-by-day life of Tevye, a dairyman, and his family. His three daughters and their courtships, plus trials and joys of village life, provide a humorous glimpse of life in pre-Revolution Russia.

This musical became the longest-running show in Broadway history when it closed on July 2, 1972, after 3,242 performances.

Some favorite songs from this musical are ''If I Were a Rich Man,'' ''Sunrise, Sunset,'' ''Miracle of Miracles'' and ''Now I Have Everything.''

NOTABLE TRIVIA

The creators of the music for this musical made love songs without using the word *love*. Affection and great caring fill the ballads . . . the sentimental songs . . . ''Miracle of Miracles,'' ''Sunrise, Sunset'' and ''Now I Have Everything.'' Quite an accomplishment!

FIDDLER ON THE ROOF
OR
"MUSIC IN THE AIR"

```
A W A R M P D A U G H T E R S
M N I S O A G G O L D E V L W
E E A S E E T N R A M M R E I
R T V T E C R C I O A I R F F
I R E O E E N R H R G O I T T
C U T S L V Y A R M O Y C I E
A S P D N M K I D F A L H B Y
E S D O A U A A M A M K I B V
E I E N O G S U N R I S E A E
F A T H E R N O I T I D A R T
```

The seven-letter Mystery Word is something the hero complained to God about quite often.

WORDS TO FIND

America, Anatevka, dances, dairyman, daughters, father, fee, fiddler, girls, gone, golde, home, left, love, mama, marriage, matchmaker, poor, rabbi, rich, ring, roof, Russia, sunrise, sunset, swift, tailor, Tevye, tradition, warm, wise

FIDDLER ON THE ROOF

Tie the information together! Social studies and music meet in these facts. Discuss, question and encourage reading and research for deeper understanding of the life of those times.

Happenings Concerning This Musical

1964—*Fiddler on the Roof* opens on September 22, 1964, at the Imperial Theater in New York City.

1971—A movie is made from this musical.

1972, July 2—*Fiddler on the Roof* closes after giving 3,242 performances.

During That Time in the United States

1964—Citizens of the District of Columbia can vote in a presidential election for the first time.

1971—Hank Aaron hits his 600th home run.

1972—*Apollo 16* and *17* make the fifth and sixth lunar landings and return to Earth successfully.

MAKING THE SUBJECT COME ALIVE
(Suggested Activities for Children)
Fiddler on the Roof

1. Read about Jewish life in Eastern Europe in the late 1800's and early 1906 era.
2. Like Tevye, create a conversation using many quotations; however, change them slightly, so they are almost wrong. Then interpret them, giving absolutely farfetched meanings.
3. Discuss tradition, its meaning . . . is it necessary? Why? Why not? Ask various people their opinions of tradition—your teacher, your principal, your parents, the manager of the local grocery store, the custodian of your school, your minister, priest or rabbi. Tell the class about your findings.
4. Listen to a recording of the songs from this musical.

NUMBER WORD GAME
Fiddler on the Roof

Refer to the story section for answers. Place the letters of your answers in the blanks after the clues. Transfer the letters to the same numbered blanks throughout the paragraph below. A story will result.

1. What was the name of the hero and his profession?

  $\overline{11}\ \overline{6}\ \overline{16}\ \overline{5}\ \overline{6}$, $\overline{20}\ \overline{8}\ \overline{7}\ \overline{18}\ \overline{5}\ \overline{19}\ \overline{8}\ \overline{12}$

2. Name the Jewish writer whose stories were the basis of this musical.

  $\overline{10}\ \overline{1}\ \overline{22}\ \overline{15}\ \overline{22}\ \overline{19}$ $\overline{8}\ \overline{15}\ \overline{6}\ \overline{7}\ \overline{3}\ \overline{1}\ \overline{6}\ \overline{19}$

3. Where is the setting of this musical and when?

  $\overline{2}\ \overline{6}\ \overline{9}\ \overline{7}\ \overline{10}\ \overline{1}$ $\overline{16}\ \overline{7}\ \overline{15}\ \overline{15}\ \overline{8}\ \overline{14}\ \overline{6}$

  $\overline{7}\ \overline{12}$ $\overline{13}\ \overline{18}\ \overline{6}\ \overline{18}\ \overline{6}\ \overline{16}\ \overline{22}\ \overline{15}\ \overline{4}\ \overline{11}\ \overline{7}\ \overline{22}\ \overline{12}$ $\overline{18}\ \overline{4}\ \overline{10}\ \overline{10}\ \overline{7}\ \overline{8}$

4. What is the name of this musical?

  $\overline{21}\ \overline{7}\ \overline{20}\ \overline{20}\ \overline{15}\ \overline{6}\ \overline{18}$ $\overline{22}\ \overline{12}$ $\overline{11}\ \overline{1}\ \overline{6}$

  $\overline{18}\ \overline{22}\ \overline{22}\ \overline{21}$

5. Name the two men who wrote the music.

  $\overline{2}\ \overline{6}\ \overline{18}\ \overline{18}\ \overline{5}$ $\overline{17}\ \overline{22}\ \overline{3}\ \overline{23}$,

  $\overline{10}\ \overline{1}\ \overline{6}\ \overline{15}\ \overline{20}\ \overline{22}\ \overline{12}$ $\overline{1}\ \overline{8}\ \overline{18}\ \overline{12}\ \overline{7}\ \overline{3}\ \overline{23}$

$\overline{11}\ \overline{6}\ \overline{16}\ \overline{5}\ \overline{6}$ $\overline{1}\ \overline{8}\ \overline{10}$ $\overline{8}$ $\overline{14}\ \overline{6}\ \overline{12}\ \overline{6}\ \overline{18}\ \overline{8}\ \overline{11}\ \overline{7}\ \overline{22}\ \overline{12}$ $\overline{14}\ \overline{8}\ \overline{13}$

$\overline{13}\ \overline{18}\ \overline{22}\ \overline{17}\ \overline{15}\ \overline{6}\ \overline{19}$ $\overline{9}\ \overline{7}\ \overline{11}\ \overline{1}$ $\overline{1}\ \overline{7}\ \overline{10}$ $\overline{20}\ \overline{8}\ \overline{4}\ \overline{14}\ \overline{1}\ \overline{11}\ \overline{6}\ \overline{18}\ \overline{10}$.

$\overline{1}\ \overline{7}\ \overline{10}$ $\overline{18}\ \overline{6}\ \overline{8}\ \overline{3}\ \overline{11}\ \overline{7}\ \overline{22}\ \overline{12}\ \overline{10}$ $\overline{11}\ \overline{22}$ $\overline{13}\ \overline{18}\ \overline{22}\ \overline{17}\ \overline{15}\ \overline{6}\ \overline{19}\ \overline{10}$,

$\overline{13}\ \overline{6}\ \overline{22}\ \overline{13}\ \overline{15}\ \overline{6}$ $\overline{8}\ \overline{12}\ \overline{20}$ $\overline{10}\ \overline{7}\ \overline{11}\ \overline{4}\ \overline{8}\ \overline{11}\ \overline{7}\ \overline{22}\ \overline{12}\ \overline{10}$,

$\overline{9}\ \overline{1}\ \overline{8}\ \overline{11}$ $\overline{1}\ \overline{6}$ $\overline{10}\ \overline{8}\ \overline{5}\ \overline{10}$ $\overline{8}\ \overline{12}\ \overline{20}$ $\overline{1}\ \overline{22}\ \overline{9}$ $\overline{1}\ \overline{6}$

$\overline{10}\ \overline{8}\ \overline{5}\ \overline{10}$ $\overline{7}\ \overline{11}$ $\overline{3}\ \overline{18}\ \overline{6}\ \overline{8}\ \overline{11}\ \overline{6}$ $\overline{8}$ $\overline{1}\ \overline{6}\ \overline{8}\ \overline{18}\ \overline{11}$

$\overline{9}\ \overline{8}\ \overline{18}\ \overline{19}\ \overline{7}\ \overline{12}\ \overline{14}$ $\overline{10}\ \overline{11}\ \overline{22}\ \overline{18}\ \overline{5}$.

CRYPTIC STORY
Fiddler on the Roof

Each story has a message in substitution code. (One letter of the alphabet has been substituted for the correct letter.) When you have discovered one word, use the known letters to help decode other words. Use the clues!

KVAMV, QVZS SN ''NLJJPVZ SB KQV ZSSN,'' QHX QLX NVVK SB KQV FZSOBJ.

ELKQ FZVHK GQHZI HBJ HB LIIVBXV HISOBK SN ELK, QV XQSEX QSE QV XVVX

KQZSOFQ KQV ILBJX SN KQV AHZLSOX GQHZHGKVZX LB KQLX

IOXLGHP. EV XVBXV LIYVBJLBF JLXHXKVZ, TOK UBSE QV ELPP TV HTPV KS

GSYV, OXLBF H QHOBKLBF, JZM XVBXV SN QOISZ.

To get you started, here are some clues. *A* is represented by *H; E* by *V; N* by *B; O* by *S;* and *T* by *K*. Good luck!

CHALLENGER CRYPTIC STORY

CUAURUG LJMTGUOTVE KXUCI VXI BIG GJRI UD CXUAUR JAITKXIR (''BIJKI MI OTVX NUY'').

XI XJC MIIG KJAAIZ ''VXI PIOTCX ZTKWIGC'' UL ''VXI PIOTCX RJLW VOJTG.'' IHTAIZ DLUR XTC GJVTFI YWLJTGI, XI ZTIZ TG GIO NULW TG 1916. VIFNI, VXI ZJTLNRJG, OJC XTC RUCV DJRUYC KXJLJKVIL.

''DTZZAIL UG VXI LUUD'' OJC MJCIZ YBUG VXI CVULTC JMUYV VIFNI JGZ XTC CIFIG ZJYQXVILC.

Here are some clues to get you started. *A* is represented by *J; E* by *I; N* by *G; O* by *U;* and *S* by *C*. Good luck!

THE MUSIC MAN

The Music Man opened December 19, 1957, at the Majestic Theater in New York City; it became the hit of the season. Meredith Willson wrote the book, music and lyrics. He made the small town of Mason City, Iowa, come alive at the turn of the century. Con man Harold Hill, a musical instrument salesman, skillfully glides from one situation to another in a most delightful style. Lively high jinks concerning musical instruments, music lessons, money and a boy that stutters have results *not* planned when love interferes.

Some favorite songs from this musical are "Seventy-six Trombones," "Good Night, My Someone," "Marian, the Librarian," and "Sales Talk."

NOTABLE TRIVIA

The melody of the catchy march "Seventy-six Trombones" appears in a different rhythm in the love song, "Good Night, My Someone."

THE MUSIC MAN
OR
"NOW YOU HEAR IT, NOW YOU DON"T"

HAROLDLOTRECNOC
SASRELDNIWSOLOA
TTPMBPEIHCRAMYC
NEUPOAOSSITMATO
EETTYNNHKAELRUP
MLSETREDSNPAALH
UFLTAEAYTRIPEKO
RALRTCRGINEHELN
TREADRHYTHMBTAY
SGWUSSENOBMORTR
NOOQUTLIBRARIAN
INCRIMINATINGNB

The nine-letter Mystery Word is
what hero Harold Hill had to cope
with time after time.

WORDS TO FIND

band, barbershop, boy, cacophony, comment, concert, disappear, Fargo, flee, Gary, happy, Harold, help, incriminating, instruments, Iowa, last, librarian, march, money, play, quartet, read, rhythm, rush, sell, solo, stutter, swindler, talk, teach, think, told, train, trombones, Wells

THE MUSIC MAN

Tie the information together! Social studies and music meet in these facts. Discuss, question and encourage reading and research for deeper understanding of the life of those times.

Happenings Concerning This Musical

1957—*The Music Man* opens on December 19, 1957, at the Majestic Theater in New York City.

1961—On April 15, 1961, *The Music Man* closes after giving 1,375 performances.

1962—Movie is made of *The Music Man* with Robert Preston and Shirley Jones.

During That Time in the United States

1957—*Mayflower II* lands at Plymouth, Massachusetts, duplicating the Pilgrim's crossing in 1620.

1961—The Indianapolis 500 auto race is won by A.J. Foyt, Jr.

1962—The Professional Golf Association voted Arnold Palmer Player of the Year.

MAKING THE SUBJECT COME ALIVE
(Suggested Activities for Children)
The Music Man

1. Listen to the opening chorus of salesmen on the train. Develop your own version of this with whatever kind of salesmen, on whatever kind of transportation you want, going wherever you wish.
2. Solve this "let's pretend" math problem. How many performances of a musical are given in a certain year (use your calendar), if there are evening performances Tuesday through Saturday night and matinees on Wednesday and Saturday afternoons?
3. Be your own version of Harold Hill. Be a car, airplane, bicycle, boat, stove, or whatever-you-want salesman even though you don't know everything about the product. Try to tell people how to drive it, all about its wonderful workings, etc.

NUMBER WORD GAME
The Music Man

Refer to the story section for answers. Place the letters of your answers on the blanks after the clues. Transfer the letters to the same numbered blanks throughout the paragraph below. A story will result.

1. Who wrote the music and lyrics? $\overline{8}\ \overline{11}\ \overline{12}\ \overline{11}\ \overline{1}\ \overline{3}\ \overline{7}\ \overline{15}\quad \overline{13}\ \overline{3}\ \overline{19}\ \overline{19}\ \overline{5}\ \overline{17}\ \overline{6}$

2. Who is the hero? $\overline{15}\ \overline{4}\ \overline{12}\ \overline{17}\ \overline{19}\ \overline{1}\quad \overline{15}\ \overline{3}\ \overline{19}\ \overline{19}$

3. Describe him. $\overline{4}\quad \overline{18}\ \overline{4}\ \overline{5}\ \overline{7}\ \overline{7}\ \overline{4}\ \overline{19}\ \overline{9}\ \overline{3}\ \overline{6}\ \overline{22}\quad \overline{8}\ \overline{24}\ \overline{5}\ \overline{3}\ \overline{16}\ \overline{4}\ \overline{19}$

   $\overline{3}\ \overline{6}\ \overline{5}\ \overline{7}\ \overline{12}\ \overline{24}\ \overline{8}\ \overline{11}\ \overline{6}\ \overline{7}\quad \overline{5}\ \overline{4}\ \overline{19}\ \overline{11}\ \overline{5}\ \overline{8}\ \overline{4}\ \overline{6}$

4. What group comments throughout the musical? $\overline{4}\quad \overline{20}\ \overline{4}\ \overline{12}\ \overline{20}\ \overline{11}\ \overline{12}\ \overline{5}\ \overline{15}\ \overline{17}\ \overline{10}$

   $\overline{25}\ \overline{24}\ \overline{4}\ \overline{12}\ \overline{7}\ \overline{11}\ \overline{7}\quad \overline{3}\ \overline{6}\quad \overline{14}\ \overline{17}\ \overline{2}\ \overline{18}\ \overline{24}\ \overline{19}$

   $\overline{15}\ \overline{4}\ \overline{12}\ \overline{8}\ \overline{17}\ \overline{6}\ \overline{3}\ \overline{26}\ \overline{3}\ \overline{6}\ \overline{22}$

5. How many trombones are there? $\overline{5}\ \overline{11}\ \overline{21}\ \overline{11}\ \overline{6}\ \overline{7}\ \overline{2}\ \overline{5}\ \overline{3}\ \overline{23}$

$\overline{15}\ \overline{4}\ \overline{12}\ \overline{17}\ \overline{19}\ \overline{1}\quad \overline{15}\ \overline{3}\ \overline{19}\ \overline{19}\quad \overline{4}\ \overline{12}\ \overline{12}\ \overline{3}\ \overline{21}\ \overline{11}\ \overline{5}\quad \overline{3}\ \overline{6}$

$\overline{12}\ \overline{3}\ \overline{21}\ \overline{11}\ \overline{12}\quad \overline{16}\ \overline{3}\ \overline{7}\ \overline{2}\quad \overline{4}\ \overline{6}\ \overline{1}\quad \overline{10}\ \overline{12}\ \overline{17}\ \overline{1}\ \overline{24}\ \overline{16}\ \overline{11}\ \overline{5}$

$\overline{16}\ \overline{2}\ \overline{16}\ \overline{19}\ \overline{17}\ \overline{6}\ \overline{3}\ \overline{16}\quad \overline{12}\ \overline{11}\ \overline{5}\ \overline{24}\ \overline{19}\ \overline{7}\ \overline{5}.\quad \overline{7}\ \overline{15}\ \overline{11}\quad \overline{7}\ \overline{17}\ \overline{13}\ \overline{6}$

$\overline{10}\ \overline{24}\ \overline{19}\ \overline{5}\ \overline{4}\ \overline{7}\ \overline{11}\ \overline{5}\quad \overline{13}\ \overline{3}\ \overline{7}\ \overline{15}\quad \overline{19}\ \overline{4}\ \overline{24}\ \overline{22}\ \overline{15}\ \overline{7}\ \overline{11}\ \overline{12},$

$\overline{5}\ \overline{17}\ \overline{6}\ \overline{22}\ \overline{5},\quad \overline{1}\ \overline{4}\ \overline{6}\ \overline{16}\ \overline{11}\ \overline{5}\quad \overline{4}\ \overline{6}\ \overline{1}\quad \overline{4}\ \overline{19}\ \overline{19}\quad \overline{5}\ \overline{17}\ \overline{12}\ \overline{7}\ \overline{5}$

$\overline{17}\ \overline{18}\quad \overline{10}\ \overline{12}\ \overline{17}\ \overline{20}\ \overline{19}\ \overline{11}\ \overline{8}\ \overline{5}.\quad \overline{24}\ \overline{5}\ \overline{24}\ \overline{4}\ \overline{19}\ \overline{19}\ \overline{2},\quad \overline{15}\ \overline{4}\ \overline{12}\ \overline{17}\ \overline{19}\ \overline{1}$

$\overline{3}\ \overline{5}\quad \overline{4}\ \overline{7}\quad \overline{7}\ \overline{15}\ \overline{11}\quad \overline{16}\ \overline{11}\ \overline{6}\ \overline{7}\ \overline{11}\ \overline{12}.$

116

CRYPTIC STORY
The Music Man

Each story has a message in substitution code. (One letter of the alphabet has been substituted for the correct letter.) When you have discovered one word, use the known letters to help decode other words. Use the clues!

"WSK BLJNH BFR" OKWJ GCC WG F VFLHGLJ JWFVW FJ F OVGLT GC WVFPKQNRO JFQKJBKR OKW GR F WVFNR. WSKNV VFTNX-CNVK HGRPKVJFWNGR NJ NRWKVJTKVJKX INWS WSK HFQQJ GC WSK HGRXLHWGV. WSK HGRPKVJFWNGR FJJLBKJ WSK WKBTG GC WSK WVFNR, PKVA JQGI FW CNVJW, NRHVKFJNRO KPKV CFJWKV FRX FW QFJW JQGINRO XGIR WG F JWGT. SNQFVNGLJ VKBFVUJ FRX MLKJWNGRJ UKKT GRK'J KFVJ JWVFNRKX JG RGWSNRO INQQ YK BNJJKX. ISFW F XKQNOSWCLQ GTKRNRO CGV F BLJNHFQ!

Good luck! To start you off, here are some letters and those that they represent. *E* is represented by *K; N* by *R; S* by *J; L* by *Q* and *A* by *F.*

CHALLENGER CRYPTIC STORY

UIZKUY MUKPYIR WIKP RIY PSRV H PIRV SR "YEK CJPSF CHR." EK YHQDP H PIRV . . . RIY KHPL YI WI. HFYJHQQL, SY SP PSCMQL PMKHDSRV SR UELYEC. IRK CJPY ZK USVEY ASYE YEK ZKHY HRW YEK IUFEKPYUH. PJWWKRQL, YEK UELYEC NJPY FHUUSKP LIJ HQIRV. PI KOMQHSRP YEK EHRWPICK CHR ASYE VUHL-VUKKR KLKP, YEK PYHU IT "YEK CJPSF CHR."

Here are some clues to start you off. *A* is represented by *H; E* by *K; N* by *R; O* by *I;* and *R* by *U.* Good luck!

118

MY FAIR LADY

My Fair Lady opened on March 15, 1956, at the Mark Hellinger Theater in New York City. This charming Cinderella story was based upon George Bernard Shaw's play *Pygmalion*. The bubbling music by Frederick Loewe and lyrics and book by Alan Jay Lerner captivated everyone.

Henry Higgins, a philologist (historical linguist) and phoneticist (expert in the sound of speech), hears a rather dirty, motley flower girl selling flowers outside fashionable Covent Garden. Her accent and way of talking is so terrible he makes notes of what she says. A challenge by his friend, Colonel Pickering, eventually leads to Eliza Doolittle taking speech lessons from Professor Henry Higgins. All sorts of problems and witty situations result as she is transformed from the dowdy, dirty flower girl into a fashionable, charming ''lady.'' The New York Company presented 2,717 performances of this musical . . . more than six years!

Some of the favorite songs from this musical are ''The Rain in Spain,'' ''Show Me,'' ''Ascot Gavotte,'' ''I've Grown Accustomed to Her Face,'' ''Get Me to the Church on Time,'' ''On the Street Where You Live,'' and ''Without You.''

NOTABLE TRIVIA
It was a smashing success in Ankara, Turkey. How interesting it would be to hear it presented in Turkish!

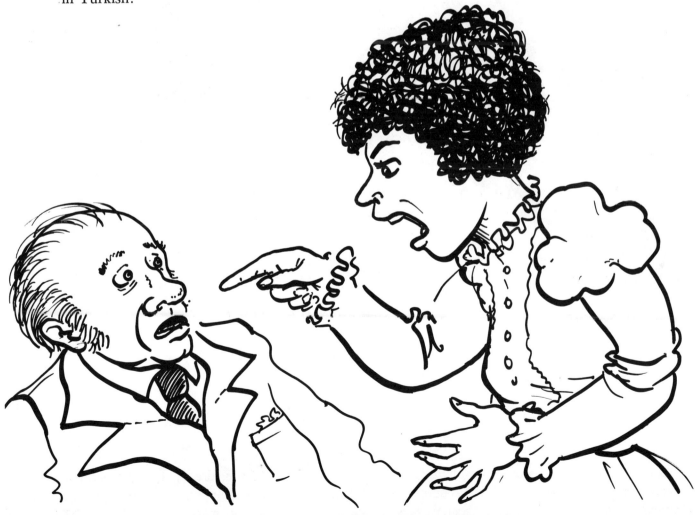

MY FAIR LADY OR "MAKE UP YOUR MIND, HENRY!"

```
D O O L I T T L E T T O V A G P
D R M R O F S N A R T S S E E N
D H E N R Y T E B E E C A R E A
E A K A L T E E R T S P F E Z I
M I N A M G E E C H N O O I D C
O F A C E S H A W N R E L R T I
T A H D E P F E C M U E V U P T
S S A R S D S T A H N O S O L E
U C R O R D I N A R Y I N U C N
C O M W S O C I E T Y T A O O O
C T E X P E R I M E N T E R R H
A N D R E W S N O I L A M G Y P
```

The ten-letter Mystery Word describes *My Fair Lady*.

WORDS TO FIND

accustomed, Andrews, ascot, atmosphere, bet, Covent, danced, Doolittle, dream, Eliza, experiment, face, Gavotte, get, harm, hats, hear, Henry, house, ideas, ordinary, performance, phonetician, pronounce, proper, *Pygmalion*, race, rain, seen, Shaw, society, speak, street, teach, transform, word

MY FAIR LADY

Tie the information together! Social studies and music meet in these facts. Discuss, question and encourage reading and research for deeper understanding of the life of those times.

Happenings Concerning This Musical

1956—On March 15, 1956, *My Fair Lady* opens at the Mark Hellinger Theater in New York City.

1962—On September 29, 1962, this musical closes after giving 2,717 performances.

1964—A motion picture is produced of *My Fair Lady,* with Rex Harrison and Julie Andrews.

During That Time in the United States

1956—Dwight D. Eisenhower is reelected President; Richard M. Nixon is reelected Vice-President.

1962—In Seattle, Washington, the World's Fair, Century 21 Exposition opens.

1964—So many people moved to California it became the state with the largest population.

MAKING THE SUBJECT COME ALIVE
(Suggested Activities for Children)
My Fair Lady

1. Read about and make a report on George Bernard Shaw.
2. Give a four or five-sentence summary of the play *Pygmalion*.
3. Discuss the ending of *My Fair Lady,* happy or unhappy? What do you think happens? Give your reasons for thinking so.
4. Listen to recordings of this musical. Make up your own version of "The Rain in Spain," for example, "I Passed the Math Test Just the Other Day,"

NUMBER WORD GAME
My Fair Lady

Refer to the story section for answers. Place the letters of your answers on the blanks after the clues. Transfer the letters to the same numbered blanks throughout the paragraph below. A story will result.

1. What is the name of the original story upon which this musical is based?

" __ __ __ __ __ __ __ __ __ "
8 4 1 16 9 10 12 2 18

2. Who wrote this story?

__ __ __ __ __ __   __ __ __ __ __ __ __   __ __ __ __
1 17 2 5 1 17   3 17 5 18 9 5 20   7 13 9 6

3. Name the man who issued a challenge to his friend Henry Higgins.

__ __ __.   __ __ __ __ __ __ __ __ __
14 2 10   8 12 14 19 17 5 12 18 1

4. What song is sung at a fashionable horse race?

" __ __ __ __ __   __ __ __ __ __ __ __ "
9 7 14 2 15   1 9 11 2 15 15 17

5. What is a phoneticist?

__ __ __ __ __ __   __ __   __ __ __
17 24 8 17 5 15   12 18   15 13 17

__ __ __ __ __   __ __   __ __ __ __ __ __
7 2 22 18 20   2 23   7 8 17 17 14 13

6. Who wrote the music?

__ __ __ __ __ __ __ __ __   __ __ __ __ __
23 5 17 20 17 5 12 14 19   10 2 17 6 17

7. Who wrote the lyrics?

__ __ __ __   __ __ __   __ __ __ __ __ __
9 10 9 18   21 9 4   10 17 5 18 17 5

__ __ __   __ __ __ __ __ __ __ __   __ __   __ __ __   __ __ __ __ __
15 13 17   14 2 16 8 2 7 17 5   2 23   15 13 17   16 22 7 12 14

__ __ __   " __ __   __ __ __ __   __ __ __ __ "   __ __ __ __.
23 2 5   16 4   23 9 12 5   10 9 20 4   22 7 17 20

__ __ __ __ __ __ __   __ __ __ __ __   __ __   __ __ __ __ __ __   __ __ __
7 17 11 17 5 9 10   15 4 8 17 7   2 23   16 22 7 12 14   23 2 5

__ __ __   __ __ __ __ __   __ __   __ __ __ __ __,   __   __ __ __ __ __ __ __,   __
15 13 17   7 2 18 1 7   9   15 9 18 1 2   9   1 9 11 2 15 15 17   9

__ __ __ __ __ __   __ __ __ __   __ __ __   __ __ __ __   __ __ __ __ __ __
8 9 15 15 17 5   7 2 18 1   9 18 20   7 2 16 17   5 9 15 13 17 5

__ __ __ __ __ __ __   __ __ __ __ __   __ __ __ __ __.
22 18 22 7 22 9 10   10 2 11 17   7 2 18 1 7

122

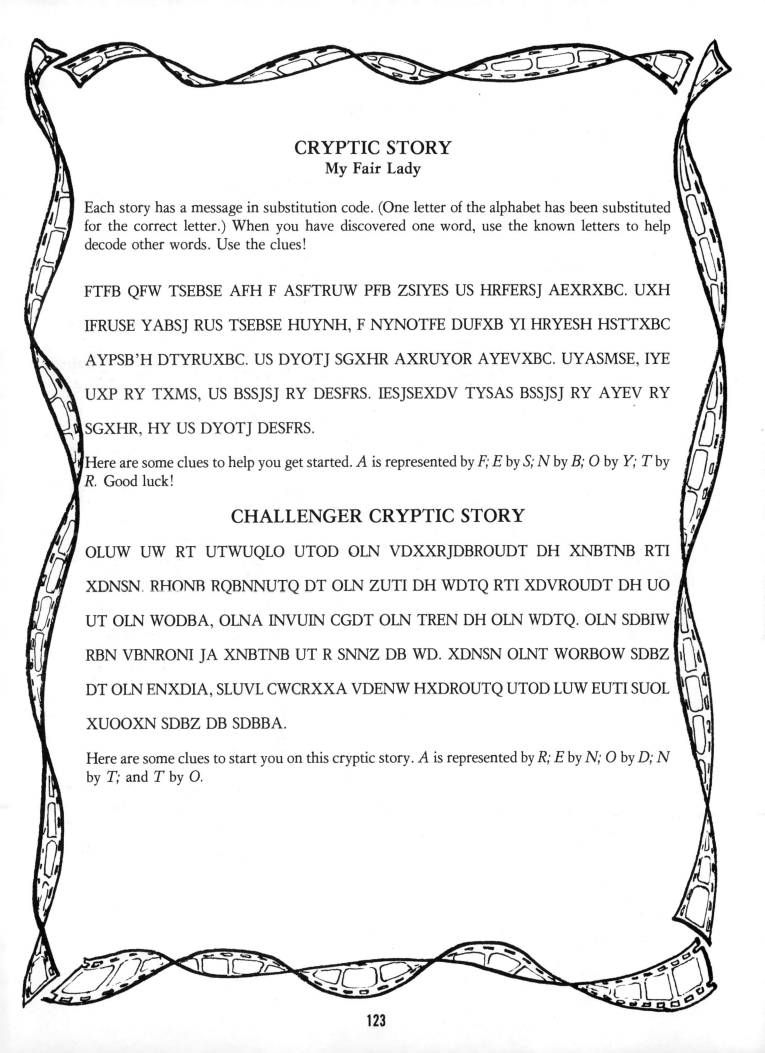

CRYPTIC STORY
My Fair Lady

Each story has a message in substitution code. (One letter of the alphabet has been substituted for the correct letter.) When you have discovered one word, use the known letters to help decode other words. Use the clues!

FTFB QFW TSEBSE AFH F ASFTRUW PFB ZSIYES US HRFERSJ AEXRXBC. UXH

IFRUSE YABSJ RUS TSEBSE HUYNH, F NYNOTFE DUFXB YI HRYESH HSTTXBC

AYPSB'H DTYRUXBC. US DYOTJ SGXHR AXRUYOR AYEVXBC. UYASMSE, IYE

UXP RY TXMS, US BSSJSJ RY DESFRS. IESJSEXDV TYSAS BSSJSJ RY AYEV RY

SGXHR, HY US DYOTJ DESFRS.

Here are some clues to help you get started. *A* is represented by *F; E* by *S; N* by *B; O* by *Y; T* by *R.* Good luck!

CHALLENGER CRYPTIC STORY

OLUW UW RT UTWUQLO UTOD OLN VDXXRJDBROUDT DH XNBTNB RTI

XDNSN. RHONB RQBNNUTQ DT OLN ZUTI DH WDTQ RTI XDVROUDT DH UO

UT OLN WODBA, OLNA INVUIN CGDT OLN TREN DH OLN WDTQ. OLN SDBIW

RBN VBNRONI JA XNBTNB UT R SNNZ DB WD. XDNSN OLNT WORBOW SDBZ

DT OLN ENXDIA, SLUVL CWCRXXA VDENW HXDROUTQ UTOD LUW EUTI SUOL

XUOOXN SDBZ DB SDBBA.

Here are some clues to start you on this cryptic story. *A* is represented by *R; E* by *N; O* by *D; N* by *T;* and *T* by *O.*

THE SOUND OF MUSIC

The Sound of Music opened November 16, 1959, at the Lunt-Fontanne Theater in New York City. It was based upon Maria von Trapp's book, *The Story of the Trapp Family Singers.* This musical completely captivated its audiences and the world in telling the warm, courageous story of Maria. She entered the Benedictine Abbey of Nonnberg with hopes of becoming a nun. However, she caused all sorts of minor disturbances, like whistling in happiness and sliding down the bannisters!

After a time, she was sent as governess for the seven children of stern, authoritative Naval hero, Captain Georg von Trapp. She brought laughter, love and music into this rigid household. Her experiences with the children, marriage to Georg, the family's narrow escape from the Nazi forces in 1939 are heart-warmingly told.

NOTABLE TRIVIA
When it was made into a movie in 1965, movie history was made. More people paid more money in more places to see this movie than ever before.

```
G M D A N C E Y E B B A C T S S
U O G O V E R N E S S U L U O I
I V S N E A R A Y A U S E N I N
T I E U N S B D L O N T G E A G
A E V N W A C Z L I J R N Z N I
R C E G R A B A A I I I I K N
E I N O H U R T P C H A W L R G
V O N T R A P P H E T C O I O G
O V E G L A V I T S E F R F W W
L M I S C H I E V O U S G E S R
```

The eight-letter Mystery Word is something Maria brought to the von Trapp family.

WORDS TO FIND

abbey, acts, Austria, baron, captain, children, dance, escape, festival, folk, governess, grin, growing, guitar, joy, life, love, low, mischievous, movie, Nazi, nine, nun, rich, rows, Salzburg, seven, singing, song, tune, Vienna, voice, von Trapp, war, wing

THE SOUND OF MUSIC

Tie the information together! Social studies and music meet in these facts. Discuss, question and encourage reading and research for deeper understanding of the life of those times.

Happenings Concerning This Musical

1959—On November 16, 1959, *The Sound of Music* opens at the Lunt-Fontanne Theater in New York City.

1963—*The Sound of Music* closes on June 15, 1962, after giving 1,443 performances.

1965—A motion picture is made of *The Sound of Music* with Julie Andrews and Christopher Plummer.

During That Time in the United States

1959—Alaska becomes the 49th state; Hawaii becomes the 50th state.

1963—Color film is developed by Polaroid.

1965—An electric power failure causes a blackout leaving many of the Northeastern states in the dark for many hours.

MAKING THE SUBJECT COME ALIVE
(Suggested Activities for Children)
The Sound of Music

1. Write to the Trapp Family Lodge in Stowe, Vermont; request a brochure and any information you may need.
2. Read Maria Ranier von Trapp's book *The Story of the Trapp Family Singers*.
3. Discover photograph books about Salzburg, Austria. Read about this city, discover other famous people who lived (or are living) there, interesting facts of its history, castles, palaces, etc.
4. Learn your favorite songs from this musical and present a program (using your class as a chorus, or a small group . . . duet, trio, etc.).

NUMBER WORD GAME
The Sound of Music

Refer to the story section for answers. Place the letters of your answers on the blanks after the clues. Transfer the letters to the same numbered blanks throughout the paragraph below. A story will result.

1. Name a song in this musical about an Alpine flower.

" __ __ __ __ __ __ __ __ __ "
  7 2 7 11 1 7 10 3 3

2. What Maria planned to become

__ __ __
4 18 4

3. How many children were in the von Trapp household?

__ __ __ __ __
3 7 20 7 4

4. Name the group of people who experienced many adventures with her.

__ __ __ __ __ __   __ __   __ __ __ __ __ __ __
22 8 16 10 11 15   9 22   6 8 21 12 8 10 4

__ __ __ __ __   __ __ __   __ __ __ __ __
17 7 9 14 17   20 9 4   12 14 8 21 21

5. Why did they leave Austria?

__ __ __ __   __ __ __ __   __ __ __ __ __
22 11 7 7   22 14 9 16   4 8 5 10 3

6. Name an inspirational song in this musical—one to give courage.

" __ __ __ __ __   __ __ __ __ __
  6 11 10 16 13   7 20 7 14 15

__ __ __ __ __ __ __ __ "
16 9 18 4 12 8 10 4

7. What did Maria bring to this family?

__ __ __ __ __ __ __ __
11 8 18 17 19 12 7 14

__ __   __ __ __ __ __ __ __,   __ __ __ __   __ __ __ __ __   __
10 4   8 16 7 14 10 6 8   12 19 7 15   13 18 10 11 12   8

" __ __ __ __ __ __ __ __ "   __ __ __ __ __ __   __ __   __ __ __ __ __,
  3 8 11 5 13 18 14 17   6 19 8 11 7 12   10 4   3 12 9 1 7

__ __ __ __ __ __ __.   __ __   __ __ __   __   __ __ __ __ __ __   __ __ __ __
20 7 14 16 9 4 12   10 12   19 8 3   8   11 9 20 7 11 15   20 10 7 1

__ __   __ __ __   __ __ __ __ __   __ __   __ __ __ __ __ __ __   __ __ __
9 22   12 19 7   19 10 11 11 3   9 22   20 7 14 16 9 4 12   8 4 2

__ __ __   __ __ __ __ __ __ __ __ __   __ __ __ __ __.   __ __ __ __
12 19 7   1 9 14 6 7 3 12 7 14   14 8 4 17 7   12 19 10 3

__ __ __ __   __ __   __   __ __ __ __ __ __ __   __ __ __ __ __ __ __ __
20 10 7 1   10 3   8   6 9 4 3 12 8 4 12   14 7 16 10 4 2 7 14

__ __   __ __ __ __ __ __   __ __ __ __ __ __ __   __ __ __ __ __ __ __.
9 22   12 19 7 10 14   13 7 11 9 20 7 2   8 18 3 12 14 10 8

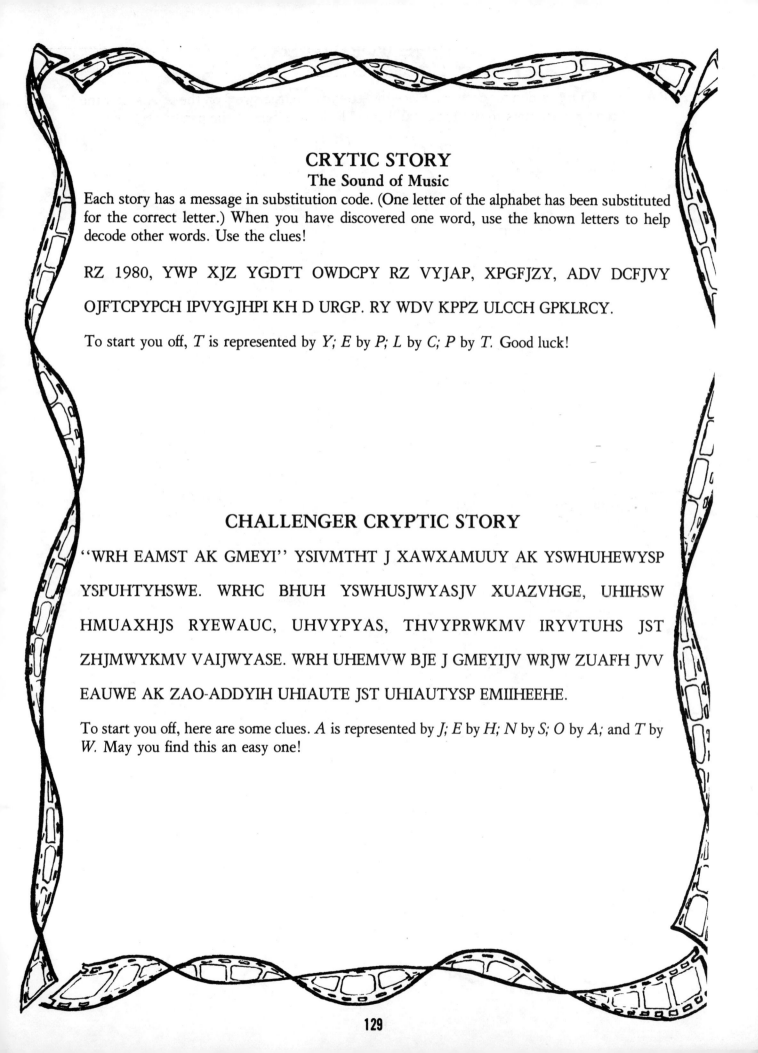

CRYTIC STORY
The Sound of Music

Each story has a message in substitution code. (One letter of the alphabet has been substituted for the correct letter.) When you have discovered one word, use the known letters to help decode other words. Use the clues!

RZ 1980, YWP XJZ YGDTT OWDCPY RZ VYJAP, XPGFJZY, ADV DCFJVY

OJFTCPYPCH IPVYGJHPI KH D URGP. RY WDV KPPZ ULCCH GPKLRCY.

To start you off, *T* is represented by *Y; E* by *P; L* by *C; P* by *T.* Good luck!

CHALLENGER CRYPTIC STORY

''WRH EAMST AK GMEYI'' YSIVMTHT J XAWXAMUUY AK YSWHUHEWYSP

YSPUHTYHSWE. WRHC BHUH YSWHUSJWYASJV XUAZVHGE, UHIHSW

HMUAXHJS RYEWAUC, UHVYPYAS, THVYPRWKMV IRYVTUHS JST

ZHJMWYKMV VAIJWYASE. WRH UHEMVW BJE J GMEYIJV WRJW ZUAFH JVV

EAUWE AK ZAO-ADDYIH UHIAUTE JST UHIAUTYSP EMIIHEEHE.

To start you off, here are some clues. *A* is represented by *J; E* by *H; N* by *S; O* by *A;* and *T* by *W.* May you find this an easy one!

ANSWER KEY

Yankee Doodle   Page 3

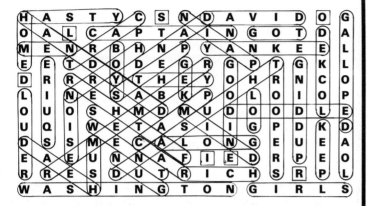

Mystery Word: Soldier

Page 5

1. "Yankee Doodle"
2. Father and I went down to camp
3. George Washington
4. Yorktown
5. unknown
6. verses

"Macaroni" was a word with several meanings. In England of the 1600's, it was a kind of knot. In Revolutionary days, it also meant "stylish."

Page 6

"Hasty pudding" was a favorite food in Colonial American homes. Whatever one had was added, usually butter, cream or milk. Often one of the following was stirred into the finished pudding: molasses, maple syrup, honey or nuts.

The Star-Spangled Banner   Page 9

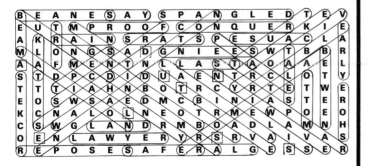

Mystery Word: Dauntless

Page 11

1. Dr. Beanes
2. War of 1812
3. September
4. Francis Scott Key
5. United States of America
6. the home of the brave
7. glad

Descendants of Francis Scott Key are living today in various states of our wonderful country.

Page 12

"The Star-Spangled Banner" has lived through much history and created many memories. "America, the Beautiful" is a calm, serene song painting a picture in words of the United States.

Occasionally, through the years, groups of Americans have suggested changing our national anthem. The melody of "The Star-Spangled Banner" has a great range, difficult interval skips and unexpected rhythmic phrases. Some of these create difficulties for the average person; however, in repeated singing these difficulties melt away.

"America, the Beautiful" is the suggested replacement. The melody, written by Samuel Ward, has a much smaller range, repeated melodic phrases and is much shorter in length. The words were written by Katherine Lee Bates in 1892, after seeing breathtaking views from the top of Pike's Peak in Colorado. These words describe America, with a special plea to God in each verse.

From the Songs of Stephen Foster
Page 15

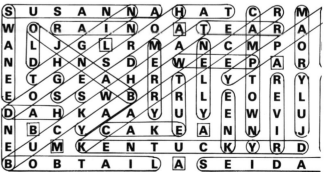

Mystery Word: Alabama

1. Lawrenceville, Pennsylvania
2. "Oh! Susanna"
3. Bardstown, Kentucky
4. Stephen Collins Foster
5. love of home and family

The old Rowan home in Bardstown, Kentucky, is where Stephen Collins Foster visited his cousins. Legend says "My Old Kentucky Home" was written here in 1853.

Page 18

When Stephen Collins Foster died in New York City, he was very poor. In his pocket was thirty-eight cents and a scrap of paper on which was written "dear friends and gentle hearts."

People were celebrating everywhere . . . it was the Fourth of July, 1826. Fifty years ago on this day, the Declaration of Independence had been signed. Sadly, two patriots who helped to create this document died on this very day, John Adams and Thomas Jefferson. On this day of happiness and grief, Stephen Collins Foster was born.

George Frideric Handel   Page 22

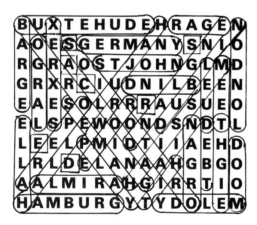

Mystery Word: Sacred

Page 24

1. Buxtehude
2. food
3. *Messiah*
4. violent temper
5. George
6. Poet's Corner in Westminster Abbey

Handel's oratorio *Messiah* was composed very rapidly. One Saturday he started writing. It was August 22, 1741. Twenty-four days later on September 14, 1741, it was completed.

Page 25

Handel was called the "Shakespeare of Music" by King George III of England. The King played the harpsichord, violin and flute and liked to play Handel's music on these instruments. Whenever a concert was presented at the palace, he insisted that some of Handel's music be on the program.

When Handel worked, he often continued through the day and night. Ideas seemed to continuously flow with ease. When food was brought for him, it remained unheeded. His ability to work was amazing.

Franz Schubert   Page 28

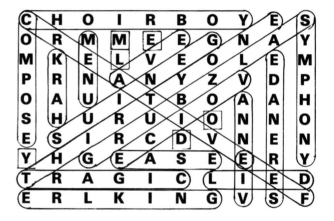

Mystery Word: Melody

Page 30

1. Franz Peter Schubert
2. January
3. extremely fast
4. Konviktschule
5. Ludwig van Beethoven

Early in May, 1809, the French bombarded Vienna. Experiencing this attack, were Franz Schubert, then twelve years old, and Ludwig Beethoven, who was twenty-six.

Page 31

Beethoven looked at about sixty of Schubert's songs during the last weeks of his life. Again and again he looked at them, repeating many times, "Truly, in Schubert there dwells a devine spark!"

Following the demise of Napoleon Bonaparte, the Metternich government tightened the rules of what one might say or write. They realized the explosive qualities and potential of words written, spoken, and sung. Intellectuals and people in the arts were closely watched and their works severely monitored.

During the year of 1814, a poet friend of Schubert's was giving a party. Suddenly, the police pounded on the door, interrupting the party. Almost everyone was taken to jail. The talented poet was kept in jail for fourteen months. Franz Schubert was released the next morning; his glasses had been broken and he had a very black eye.

Giuseppe Verdi   Page 34

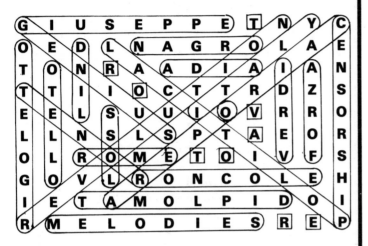

Mystery Word: Trovatore

Page 36

1. Le Roncole, Italy
2. village innkeeper
3. *Nabucco*
4. freedom
5. wonderful, singable melodies
6. hated invaders

When Verdi completed an opera, he planted a tree. Some are a plane tree for *Rigoletto,* an oak for *Il Trovatore,* a willow for *La Traviata.*

Page 37

While working on his second opera, Verdi's two young sons died; then his wife died. This tragedy desolated him completely; it seemed no music remained in his soul. A friend encouraged him; finally, he wrote *Nabucco.* This opera gave hope to Italians, hope for freedom from the invading Austrian army. Verdi became their hero and was greatly loved the rest of his life.

When Verdi was nineteen years old, he applied for entrance to the Milan Conservatory of Music. His application was rejected. Reasons later discovered—Conservatory overcrowded, he was a foreigner, too old and did not hold hands correctly in piano playing. Years later, the Conservatory wanted to be named after him. Verdi answered their request for this permission by remarking, "They wouldn't have me young. They cannot have me old." It was later named for him.

Peter Tchaikovsky   Page 40

Mystery Word: Masterpiece

Page 42

1. Peter Ilich Tchaikovsky
2. *Pathétique*
3. French, German
4. November

In 1890, Tchaikovsky went to New York City. He was stunned by the skyscrapers. He is said to have commented, "What are people thinking of to live on the thirteenth floor of a building?"

Page 43

Composers make use of all they see and hear and through their own creative genius make it their own. Tchaikovsky used folk melodies in this way. From his writings, he has told us the source of some of these ideas.

A song he frequently heard sung by blind beggars on the street became a theme in his *Concerto in B flat minor and Piano, No. F, Opus 23.* A friend's butler was singing a popular folk melody called "The Crane." It appears in the finale of his *Symphony No. 2 in C minor, Opus 17.*

Peter Tchaikovsky and French composer Camille Saint-Saëns were invited to England to receive a doctorate from Cambridge University. Saint-Saëns called him the ''gentlest and kindest of men,'' also remarking that he was a composer of ''talent and astounding technique.''

John Philip Sousa   Page 46

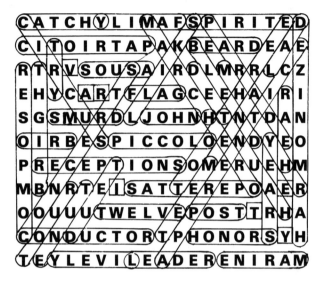

Mystery Word: Variety

Page 48

1. Washington, D.C.
2. fourteen
3. Conductor of the Marine Band
4. The March King
5. John Philip Sousa
6. white kid gloves
7. Pennsylvania

Returning by ship from Europe in 1896, John Philip Sousa strolled about the deck. A melody floated into his mind as he saw ''Old Glory'' flying at the stern of the ship. It developed into ''The Stars and Stripes Forever.''

Page 49

John Philip Sousa's father's name was Antonio So (his family was Spanish). A story is told that John Philip Sousa added U.S.A. to it; thus the name Sousa was created.

Some composer's music is instantly recognized—a waltz by Johann Strauss II, a composition by Wolfgang Amadeus Mozart or a march by John Philip Sousa. Through their very own talents, they created a style and individuality that was distinctively their own. Sousa's marches have a verve, zest and spirit that lift our emotions. He raised the march and band music to heart-stirring heights.

Sergei Prokofiev   Page 52

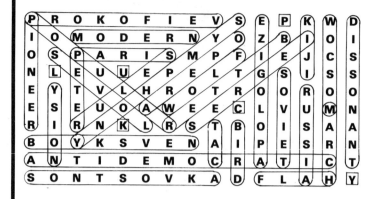

Mystery Word: Plucky

Page 54

1. Sontsovka, Russia
2. St. Petersburg Conservatory of Music
3. *Peter and the Wolf*
4. Central Committee of the Communist Party

Peter and the Wolf was written in one week. He conducted this orchestral work at its first performance at an afternoon concert for children on May 2, 1936, at the Children's Theater in Moscow.

Page 55

Wherever he went, Prokofiev carried notebooks to write ideas, melodies and themes of music. Sometimes they came when he was eating, walking, in bed or anywhere! When he started a new composition, these were invaluable. Generally, he composed between ten in the morning and noon.

When Prokofiev was working, he liked to have some candy on his desk. He always carried some in his pockets. He was always trying and creating new things. Some were successful, some failures. One unusual creation was a new way of writing—without vowels!

Mikhail Baryshnikov   Page 59

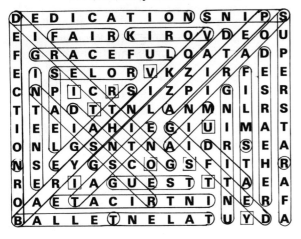

Mystery Word: Virtuosity

Page 61

1. Mikhail Baryshnikov
2. Riga, Latvia
3. International Ballet Competition
4. twenty-six
5. Artistic Director of the American Ballet Theatre
6. soaring leaps and jumps

When he retires from dancing, "Misha" plans to enjoy his home in Connecticut. He has two dogs, a golden retriever named Katia and a black poodle named Goulue.

Page 62

At one time when he was living in Leningrad, he had a nice apartment on the Moika Canal. Russian poet Alexander Pushkin had lived right across the way during the last days of his life.

Mikhail sometimes smokes a pipe. In 1979, he received an Honorary Doctorate of Fine Arts from Yale. James Cagney is his hero.

Luciano Pavarotti   Page 65

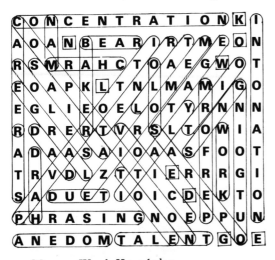

Mystery Word: Knowledge

Page 67

1. Luciano Pavarotti
2. Modena, Italy
3. white handkerchief
4. all over the world
5. *Yes, Giorgio!*
6. bent nail

Luciano Pavarotti likes to drive cars very fast. A friend cautioned him if the police caught him, his driver's license would be taken away. Luciano is said to have replied, "They can't. I don't have one!"

Page 68

Whenever traveling on an airplane, Pavarotti buys an economy priced ticket. He does not believe in the frivolous "extras" included in first class.

Luciano Pavarotti owns two homes. One is in Modena, the city of his birth and boyhood. In 1974, he bought a seaside house in Pesaro, the lovely old town on the Adriatic Sea. Now it is renovated and modernized to the Pavarotti family needs. Each summer the Pavarottis escape to lose themselves in family life . . . an interlude to remember.

Itzhak Perlman   Page 71

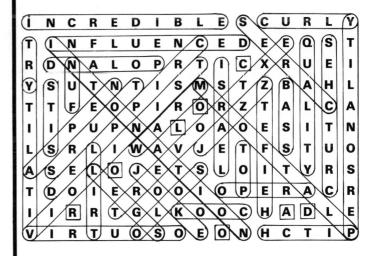

Mystery Word: Colorado

Page 73

1. Itzhak Perlman
2. violin
3. Jascha Heifetz
4. extraordinary courage
5. Aspen, Colorado
6. witty, debonaire

As a thirteen-year-old, in 1958, Itzhak traveled on an "Ed Sullivan Caravan of Stars" tour. This Israeli native and his family later moved to New York City. There he continued his musical education.

Page 74

Itzhak Perlman and his wife, Toby, have four children. They have a home in the country in upstate New York. In New York City, their eleven-room apartment has a view of the Hudson River. This apartment once belonged to Babe Ruth.

Itzhak loves to eat. He is a gourmet cook. His bass voice was heard in the one-line part of a jailer, on a TV production. With conductor-composer Andre Previn, he recorded some of Scott Joplin's rags.

Mstislav Rostropovich   Page 77

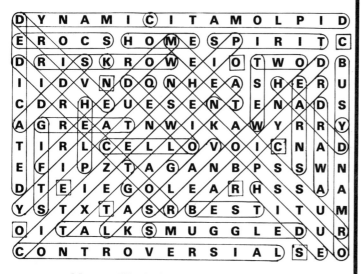

Mystery Word: Concertos

Page 79

1. Mstislav Rostropovich
2. Baku, Russia
3. joyous
4. cello
5. extraordinary talent

Famous people played "toy" instruments. The orchestra was led by Franz Joseph Haydn (alias Rostropovich) in *The Toy Symphony*. Unexpected fun and much laughter was the result.

Page 80

"Buttercup" was the name given to a land-rover van Mstislav and Galina Rostropovich bought in England. Mstislav found a horn that "mooed" like a cow. They installed it in the land-rover. Back to Moscow they drove, mooing all the way across Europe, much to the puzzlement of local cows.

Mstislav has a tiny dog that has long taffy-colored hair. He often brings him to orchestra rehearsals when he is the cello soloist. As Rostropovich performs on his cello, the tiny dog sits quietly under his master's chair. He seems to recognize the final cadence, for he immediately jumps up and runs between the rows of the string section, barking happily all the time.

Andrés Segovia   Page 83

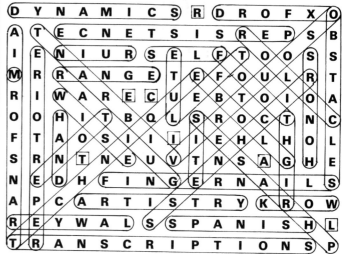

Mystery Word: Recital

Page 85

1. Andrés Segovia
2. Linares, Spain
3. extraordinary, fabulous technique
4. "Work . . . when water is still, it becomes stagnant."

Segovia was swimming in the Mediterranean Sea when he became aware of a huge shadow following him. A shark! A motor boat was sent to rescue him. Finally, at the boat, a reassuring voice called, "It's a dolphin being friendly!" What a relief!

Page 86

The first concerto for guitar composed in the twentieth century was written by Italian composer Mario Castelnuovo-Tedesco for Segovia. The *Concerto in D major* has been described as "bittersweet."

Assorted comments by Segovia . . . "The sound of the guitar on record does not have the delicacy, the poetry, and nuance present in the instrument's live sound." . . . "The electric guitar robs the guitar of its poetry and delicious sound." . . . About today's avant-garde writing . . . "They write pieces with sounds . . . oop, eeep, ahhh . . . and call that music. It is not."

Beverly Sills   Page 89

Mystery Word: Heartbreak

Page 91

1. Beverly Sills
2. coloratura soprano
3. Brooklyn, New York
4. Five different universities gave her an honorary doctor's degree.
5. joyous, bubbling, happiness

There are various types of soprano voices. The coloratura voice is a high clear voice capable of producing all sorts of trills and fancy ornamental notes.

Page 92

The performance was going well as Beverly sang beautifully, carrying a small dog in her arms. Suddenly, she became aware of something warm and very wet spreading from the dog; she immediately put him down. He began to howl and her solo became a duet for the remainder of her aria. The audience loved the unexpected action.

At La Scala Opera House, Beverly requested a costume remade in silver for a role she was to sing. The management said "Yes." Nothing happened. Another request . . . nothing happened. Still another request . . . still nothing. Finally, she folded the costume neatly, took scissors and carefully cut it in half. She got her costume in silver.

Joan Sutherland   Page 95

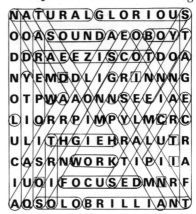

Mystery Word: Diction

Page 97

1. Joan Sutherland
2. Sydney, Australia
3. Royal Conservatory of Music, London, England
4. Richard Bonynge
5. vocal technique

Joan Sutherland is taller than many operatic heroines. She is human and does like to be comfortable. She enjoys having her shoes off.

Page 98

Learning how to fall is one of the techniques of stagecraft. She learned rapidly. Then, with impish delight, this stately lady would become utterly limp and crash backwards on the floor.

Joan Sutherland will only sing if her husband, Richard Bonynge, conducts the orchestra. His wise advice has guided their work together for thirty-three years. They have a home in Montreux, Switzerland, called "Les Avants."

Annie   Page 102

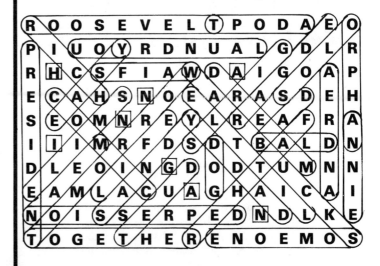

Mystery Word: Hannigan

Page 104

1. Annie, Sandy
2. Daddy Warbucks
3. millionaire
4. brave, optimistic

A thirteen-year-old was the first ''Annie.'' Andrea McArdle's blue-gray eyes shined as she made her acting debut. The orphans and Annie had to be replaced as they grew up.

Page 105

Sometimes problems with animals arise. The dog playing ''Sandy'' ran away; consternation and confusion reigned. Finally, he returned on his own.

The summer before *Annie* appeared on Broadway, Sandy appeared in the Connecticut version. He did follow the director's suggestions . . . most of the time. In one scene Annie and Sandy were to be chased off the stage by police. Sandy changed the action by chasing the police off the stage . . . not once but for several performances.

Fiddler on the Roof   Page 108

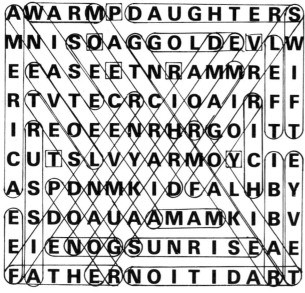

Mystery Word: Poverty

Page 110

1. Tevye, dairyman
2. Sholom Aleichem
3. Jewish village in pre-Revolution Russia
4. *Fiddler on the Roof*
5. Jerry Bock, Sheldon Harnick

Tevye has a generation gap problem with his daughters. His reactions to problems, people and situations, what he says and how he says it create a heartwarming story.

Page 111

Tevye, hero of *Fiddler on the Roof,* has his feet on the ground. With great charm and an immense amount of wit, he shows how he sees through the minds of the various characters in this musical. We sense impending disaster, but know he will be able to cope, using a haunting, dry sense of humor.

Solomon Rabinowitz chose the pen name of Sholom Aleichem (''peace be with you''). He has been called ''The Jewish Dickens'' or ''The Jewish Mark Twain.'' Exiled from his native Ukraine, he died in New York in 1916. Tevye, the dairyman, was his most famous character. *Fiddler on the Roof* was based upon the stories about Tevye and his seven daughters.

The Music Man   Page 114

Mystery Word: Situation

Page 116

1. Meredith Willson
2. Harold Hill
3. a fast-talking musical instrument salesman
4. a barbershop quartet in joyful harmonizing
5. seventy-six

Harold Hill arrives in River City and produces cyclonic results. The town pulsates with laughter, songs, dances and all sorts of problems. Usually, Harold is at the center.

The Music Man gets off to a raucous start as a group of traveling salesmen get on a train. Their rapid-fire conversation is interspersed with the calls of the conductor. The conversation assumes the tempo of the train, very slow at first, increasing ever faster and at last slowing down to a stop. Hilarious remarks and questions keep one's ears strained so nothing will be missed. What a delightful opening for a musical!

Robert Preston does not sing a song in *The Music Man*. He talks a song . . . not easy to do. Actually, it is simply speaking in rhythm. One must be right with the beat and the orchestra. Suddenly, the rhythm just carries you along. So explains the handsome man with gray-green eyes, the star of *The Music Man*.

My Fair Lady   Page 120

Mystery Word: Delightful

Page 122

1. *Pygmalion*
2. George Bernard Shaw
3. Col. Pickering
4. "Ascot Gavotte"
5. expert in the sound of speech
6. Frederick Loewe
7. Alan Jay Lerner

The composer of the music for *My Fair Lady* used several types of music for the songs—a tango, a gavotte, a patter song and some rather unusual love songs.

Alan Jay Lerner was a wealthy man before he started writing. His father owned The Lerner Shops, a popular chain of stores selling women's clothing. He could exist without working. However, for him to live, he needed to create. Frederick Loewe needed to work to exist, so he could create.

This is an insight into the collaboration of Lerner and Loewe. After agreeing on the kind of song and location of it in the story, they decide upon the name of the song. The words are created by Lerner in a week or so. Loewe then starts work on the melody, which usually comes floating into his mind with little work or worry.

The Sound of Music   Page 126

Mystery Word: Laughter

Page 128

1. "Edelweiss"
2. nun
3. seven
4. family of Captain Georg von Trapp
5. flee from Nazis
6. "Climb Every Mountain"
7. laughter

In America, they built a "Salzburg" chalet in Stowe, Vermont. It has a lovely view of the hills of Vermont and the Worcester Range. This view is a constant reminder of their beloved Austria.

Page 129
In 1980, the von Trapp chalet in Stowe, Vermont, was almost completely destroyed by a fire. It has been fully rebuilt.

The Sound of Music included a potpourri of interesting ingredients. They were international problems, recent European history, religion, delightful children and beautiful locations. The result was a musical that broke all sorts of box-office records and recording successes.